Taking Charge
Missy's Way

Taking Charge Missy's Way

Patricia Bullock

Library of Congress Control Number:		2018915017
ISBN:	Hardcover	978-1-9845-7365-0
	Softcover	978-1-9845-7364-3
	eBook	978-1-9845-7363-6

Print information available on the last page.

Rev. date: 12/21/2018

To order additional copies of this book, contact:
Xlibris
1-888-795-4274
www.Xlibris.com
Orders@Xlibris.com
786340

It was a beautiful day. The sun was shining, and the day was warm. It was Mother's Day, and I was sitting in a small café in Kleene, Texas, thinking about how much I missed my mom. I was ordering lunch and coffee when I got a call from my friend George. I answered my phone. "Hello, George, I'm on the way home. I planned on stopping by on the way to the apartment. Is everything okay?"

George replied, "Yes, but I need to talk to you. How far away are you?"

"About an hour or so. I'll bring dinner when I arrive, okay?"

"You don't have to take care of me, you know. But if you want to bring dinner, I won't complain." He chuckled. "Be careful," he said and then hung up.

George is such a sweet man. I remember the day George came into my life as if it were only yesterday instead of three years ago. He's an older gentleman. He's an attorney who had retired but still does some work from his home.

I met him one tragic day in March of 1982. I was returning home from a weekend ride with some friends when we came upon a traffic accident. A gray Cadillac had gone off the road into a tree. I called 911 and rushed to help, but sadly, the woman driving wasn't breathing, and the man had hit his head on the windshield and was bleeding. I pulled the door open and pulled the lady out and started CPR, and Joe and Charlee pulled the gentleman out of the car and were trying to calm him down as he was frantic about his wife. I felt the lady's heartbeat, but it was faint.

The ambulance showed up and took over, and I went over to help the gentleman. He had a broken arm, and blood was pouring from his head. Even though he was in pain, all he wanted to do was get to his wife. I helped hold him back while they worked on his wife, and a second ambulance showed, so I helped him get into it and told him that he would see her at the hospital. I asked his name, and he told me it was George and his wife was Sophie. He looked so lost that I offered to ride with him to the hospital. He was so upset and worried that I just couldn't let him go by himself.

I told Joe and Charlee to go home and I would call them later. I told George that they were taking great care of her, but he needed to get to the hospital so he could see his wife. He asked me to check on his wife, so I walked over, and the EMT shook his head and said it would be a miracle if she pulled through. I went back to George, and I told him they were working on her; they were doing everything they could, and they were heading to the hospital. He had tears running down his face. I asked if I could ride with him, and the EMT said yes. I held his hand while they cleaned up his head and put a brace on his arm. They wrapped his ribs, and they wanted to start an IV, but George said not until he saw his wife. He told them that until he knew if she was okay, only then would he get treatment, so we went to the hospital, and they helped him in a wheelchair. I told them I'd take care of him. The EMT talked to the nurse, and they said that he could go see his wife. I knew then that she must have not made it. I pushed George into a room, and a nurse and a doctor was there. George saw his wife, and he cried. The doctor said they did everything possible, but her heart had given out. They suspect that she had a heart attack while driving, and that was what caused the accident. I stayed with George until he was ready to leave. I insisted he get checked out by the doctors, and then I would take him home. I stayed with him while the doctors check him out. He had a concussion, broken ribs, a broken arm, and a deep cut on his forehead, and he needed to have stitches. The nurses and the doctor were worried about how he was going to handle losing his wife, so they kept him overnight. I stayed until they got him to his room, and I told him I'd be back to check on him in the morning. He said it didn't matter; nothing mattered now. I rode back to the accident scene and got my bike and went back to the hospital. They gave George something to help him sleep and something to help with pain, so he was sleeping when I got there. He looked so pale, and you could tell he was in pain by the look on his face as he slept. I decided that I'd stay in case he needed anything through the night. I slept on and off through the night in the chair in his room.

The next morning, he was surprised to see me, but I told him I'd be there for him. He thanked me for everything and told me I didn't have to bother with an old man. He said he would be okay; he just had to figure out how to live without his Sophie. I stayed with him most of the day, and they released him around dinnertime. I asked him if he had any children I could call, but he said his only son James passed away in a motorcycle accident when he was in his early twenties. He didn't talk much, and when a social worker came in to talk to him about being discharged and about his wife, he got upset, so I talked to the social worker in the hallway and told her that I'd be helping him with anything he needed. The nurse came in with discharge papers, and I signed everything, and then I called a cab for George. I walked him out to the cab and got his address and gave it to the driver. I asked George if I could come and check on him, and he said I could, but I didn't have to. I gave him a hug and told him to call me if he needed anything. I gave him my number and told him I'd see him later. I checked on him several times over the next few days, and we became friends and then later a family. I offered to help with the funeral arrangements, and he thanked me. He seemed lost, and I knew that he needed me, so I was there at every chance I could check on him, bring him food, and take him to places he needed to go. He had a really bad time on the day of the funeral, but I stayed by his side. There were a lot of people at the service expressing their sympathy, but George was in shock over his loss. There were cards, flowers, and gifts; and he didn't know what to do with them. He told the priest that I would know what to do with them, so I told him I'd take care of it. He said that he didn't want any of the flowers or gifts, and he asked me to give them instead to the women's shelter that was Sophie's favorite. He had a lot of ups and downs over the following weeks and months, but as the year went on, George adjusted to living without Sophie. Nevertheless, he missed her so much, and he talked of her often.

He not only became my friend but my family also, since I didn't have any family to speak of. George didn't like me riding my Harley, but he eventually got used to it. He would fuss and always had me call him so he could check on me in my rides. He became a father to me, since I didn't have much of one while growing up. When I got to George's house, he let me know I got a certified letter from an attorney in Pennsylvania. I told him to open it and tell me what it was about. I figured it was from my father or my evil stepmother. I didn't give a hoot about either of them, but I had sent my dad my address in case he needed something. I never heard from him though, and I had used George's address so they wouldn't know my exact address. I stopped and rode the subway, and then I went to George's house.

George told me to sit down and eat first, and then he would go over the letter with me. George read the letter to me, and apparently, my father and stepmother was killed in a car accident. The letter said that alcohol was involved, but it didn't say which of the two was drinking or if anybody else was involved. The accident happened over six months ago just before Thanksgiving, but the news only just got to me, but then I didn't keep up with them or talk to them in over five years. The letter instructed me to contact them for information about the will and the arrangements, but since it took this long, I told George to throw the letter away. They were already dead and buried, and I didn't want anything of theirs anyway. George read the rest of the letter to himself, and then he paused and said, "There is a child involved, Missy. You have a baby brother and you are appointed his guardian."

"How could there be a child? My father didn't take care of me when I was a child, so how could he have another child?" I said. "He wasn't a father material then, and neither was stepmommy. She was a horrible person, and I can't imagine her even wanting children."

"I know you're in shock, but you need to contact this law firm and find out about this boy. He is your brother," George said.

"He's not my responsibility," I said, but George reminded me how I took care of him and said that he knew I'd change my mind. He told me to think about it tonight and we'd talk about it tomorrow.

Once I got home, I checked my mail and wrote out my electric and water bill. I walked over to check on Sally, my neighbor. She worried about me on my bike and, thus, liked it when I check in. Sally was glad I came home safe; she had saved me a plate of meat loaf, fried potatoes, onions, and a slice of her lemon cake. I thanked her and told her I would pick her up at eight thirty a.m. for breakfast. Sally liked going to the market on Tuesdays because it was senior day, and she could save more on groceries. I always made sure to be at home on Tuesdays so that I could take her to breakfast and go shopping with her.

I took a shower and put on my pajamas, and I heated up the dinner that Sally gave me. She was a great cook, and she was so kind. She was the first person I met when I moved here, and everyone else had come and gone, except me and Sally. She was like a mother to me. If I was doing something she didn't approve of, she would tell me; if she didn't like what I was wearing, she would tell me so; and if I didn't call her, she would call me. I was very lucky to have her and George in my life.

As I was eating, I heard a meow sound out of my kitchen window, so I went outside, and there was this tiny kitten. It was wet from Sally's flower garden that she watered earlier, and so I brought it in and wrapped it in a towel. I dried it off and gave it some milk, and it sat on my lap while I ate and watched TV. It was so little, and I was afraid to put it back outside, so I let it sleep with me. I kept calling it, "Hey, you," so I decided to call it Tabby. It was mostly white with orange feet and face. It reminded me of my cat that I had growing up, but I had to give it away because when Dad got married, his wife said she was allergic to cats, although she played with the neighbor's cat when she was over there visiting. Obviously, she just wanted to make my life hell, and she did. Dad wanted to give me his car, but she said I needed to learn responsibility and that I needed a job so that I could buy it. "Nothing is free," she said. I wanted a high school ring, but she wouldn't let Dad pay for it. She told me if I wanted one, it was my responsibility, and my dad never said a word; he didn't even come see me graduate because she had lunch plans with friends, and she said it would be rude to cancel. When I think of everything that witch put me through, I'm glad she's dead. I moved out as soon as I graduated and never went back. My father chose her over me in everything, so the day I graduated, I took all my money out of the bank and bought me a used Harley Davidson, packed what few things I could take with me, and went to Texas. I wanted to be as far away from them as I could be, so I left and never looked back. That was six years ago, and I wrote Dad a letter and gave him my address and phone number. He never called or written, not even for my birthdays, so I quit caring.

After a restless night, I got up irritable, but playing with Tabby helped get me a better mood. I gave her some milk, and while she drank her milk, I went over to Sally's apartment and asked her if she knew where the kitten came from. She said the people who moved out last week left the mother cat and its kittens in the apartment, and when Danny came to paint and clean, most of the kittens were dead and the mother escaped. He put the two kittens out, hoping someone would take them, but one got run over yesterday. I asked her if she would help me take care of Tabby since I was always on the go, and she said she would help me look after Tabby when I was gone riding or gone overnight somewhere. I took Sally to Mike's diner for breakfast—they had the best pancakes—and I told Sally about the letter and this little boy. I told her, "I don't know how to take care of a little kid. Hell, I can barely take care of myself."

Sally laughed. "You take care of yourself just fine. Plus, you take care of me and George. Missy, you're a good person, and I bet this little innocent boy would be happy to have you care for him. After all, he is your brother. You just can't pick and choose your family," Sally said, and then she smiled widely. "And you'll have help from me and George. We'll always be there for you like you're here for us."

I smiled. "You and George are easy, but a three-year-old . . . I have no idea how to take care of him, but thank you." I gave Sally a hug.

I took Sally shopping for groceries, and I picked up kitten food, litter, litter box, and toys. I found Tabby a collar and a leash, and then after I got Sally home and unloaded the stuff we bought, I helped her put her groceries away. Then I went home and took care of Tabby. After I got everything done, I went to see George and saw what I needed to do to find out about a child who was possibly my sibling. I took George out to a late lunch and coffee, and I asked him what I needed to do to find out about this child. He said he had already called and told the lawyer that he was my attorney, and they gave him all the information and sent a copy of the will by e-mail. George read all of the will to me and all the information on the house property, as well as information on my baby brother Nickolas Robert Chambers. He was four years old, and he had a nanny, housekeeper, and head housekeeper to care for him until the time I come and take over. There was also an uncle at the house running things until I arrive. Everything was left to me and Nickolas, and I was his guardian and trustee until he gets to the age of nineteen, and I was made conservator over his inheritance until he gets twenty-five years old. After talking with George, he persuaded me to go to Pennsylvania to meet the boy and decide what to do. I asked George to come with me, but he said he would be at my disposal if I needed him.

I called my friend Shelly. I get her to help out George and Sally at times when I'm not available. I pay her to help with them in shopping and taking them to the doctors when I can't be there. I went home and asked Sally if she could keep Tabby while I was away and that Shelly would be around if she needed anything. I made calls and paid all my bills up for two months, and I called Shelly to help Sally out and take her to the grocery and to her doctor's appointment. I also asked her to do the same for George. She had helped me out several times with them, but she didn't have a car, so I left her my car for her to use. I called and added her on the insurance and left her with $500 that she could use as she saw fit. George wasn't happy about hiring a baby sitter, but I explained that it was Shelly and that I'd be back as soon as I could. He wasn't happy that I was driving across the country on my bike, but I told him I'd check with him several times a day. George called the attorney and informed them that I'd be there one day next week. I left on Friday morning after saying my goodbyes to Sally and George.

I traveled on good weather for most of the drive, and it took me four days to get to Galantine, Texas, and it rained most of the last day, so I was behind schedule. Thus, I called the house and told them I'd be in after dark that night. The housekeeper Mrs. Tinsley didn't seem to be impressed that I called, but she said my room would be ready whenever I showed up. I ran into a hailstorm which put me getting there around three in the morning. I was wet, cold, and tired when I arrived, and I checked under the flower pot on the front porch to see if there was still a key, and there was. Lucky for me, it worked. I guess Dad was too cheap to change locks after I left. I let myself in quietly so I wouldn't disturb anyone, but I guess my Harley woke up the butler because when I went in the house, he grabbed me and threw me on the floor before turning on the light. I hit the floor hard, and it knocked the breath out of me. When the lights came on, there was a man in his mid-thirties looming over me, and I was as startled as he was. "What the hell? Who are you, and why are you breaking in my house?" he growled.

"Excuse me, this is my house, and who are you?" I asked.

His face softened. "You're Melissa Chambers. Why are you sneaking in the middle of the night? We expected you earlier today," he said as he helped me up. "Are you hurt? Sorry about that, but you should have called if you were going to be this late."

"Yes, I'm fine, and I did call and spoke to a Mrs. Tinsley. I got caught in the rain and a hailstorm, so I had to pull off and wait the storm out, that's why. And who are you?"

"I'm Robert Williams. My mother married your father. Sorry about throwing you in the floor. Are you sure you're okay?" he asked.

"Yes, I'm fine, just cold and wet mainly." Just then, I noticed several people watching.

"So sorry. Let me introduce you to Mrs. Tinsley, the head housekeeper; Ms. Trina, your maid; and Charles is the butler."

"Nice to meet you all, but can we do this again in the morning? I'd like to get into something dry and get some sleep."

"Of course. Trina, can you help Melissa to her room? I'll see you in the morning," Robert said.

Trina showed me to my room. It was the same as when I lived here. The same curtains, bedspread, and rugs on the floor. In the dresser and closets were my clothes that I left behind. Trina offered me a hot bath, but I thanked her and said I just needed some sleep, so she said good night and left. I stripped off my wet clothes, climbed into my bed with nothing on, and fell asleep instantly.

I woke up early, showered, put on a pair of jeans and a white T-shirt, and went downstairs to find coffee. There was a sweet old lady cooking breakfast, and I introduced myself. "Hi. I'm Missy Chambers. Can I have a cup of coffee?"

She smiled and said, "Of course, you can. Let me get you a cup. I'm Margaret. I'm the cook. Mrs. Chambers hired me five years ago." She poured me a cup, and I told her about my entrance last night, and we laughed. "Good thing you weren't hurt. Those marble floors aren't very soft." Margaret said.

"No, they're not. When I was growing up, they had carpet, but I guess Dad updated after I left. What time does my baby brother come down for breakfast? I'm anxious to meet him."

"His nanny comes down and makes his food and feeds him in the nursey."

"I thought the lawyers said he's three. Why is he in a nursey still?"

"Your father would bring him down to breakfast when he was here, but since he's passed, the nanny rules."

"Well, that's ridiculous. He's not a baby. I'll go up and bring him down. I'll be right back."

I went upstairs and knocked on several doors. An old woman opened one of the doors, and she asked, "What do you want?"

"Is this the nursey?"

"Yes, I'm Mrs. Conner. What do you want?" the lady said.

"I want to meet my brother, I'm Melissa Chambers."

"I haven't let him up yet. You'll have to wait until later," Mrs. Conner said as she went to shut the door, but I pushed the door open, and here's this little boy lying in a crib.

I walked passed the lady and said, "Hi, I'm Missy. I'm your big sister. Do you want to come and have breakfast with me?"

The little boy smiled, said "Yes," and started to get up, but the woman said, "No you can't. You don't get up until nine, and then I'll feed you your cereal."

I turned to the woman and looked her in the face. "I'm taking him downstairs. Please move out of my way." I picked him up and started downstairs.

The nanny said, "Excuse me, I'm the caretaker here, not you. I'll be talking to Mr. Williams about this."

"Go ahead. He's not my boss, and Nicky isn't in your care anymore. You're fired."

"You can't fire me. You have no rights in this house, only Mr. Williams does," she said, but I walked on without saying anything. I went to the kitchen, and Margaret was at the sink. She turned and smiled. "Hello, little one." She handed Nicky a cinnamon roll. Nicky took it and ate it like he hadn't been fed for days.

I asked Margaret, "He acts like he's starving. Can we fix him some scramble eggs and maybe bacon and toast?"

"Mrs. Conner fixes him mush most of the time. He probably hasn't even had eggs and bacon before. She won't even feed him my meatloaf and mashed potatoes. She insists that she knows what's best." Margaret rolled her eyes, and I started laughing.

"Well, she has no say anymore. I fired her."

Margaret's eyes got big, and she smiled. "I think I like you. Now go out to the dining table, and I'll bring breakfast out to you in a few."

I took Nicky out to the table and sat him in a chair. I sat beside him. "Are you hungry?" I asked.

Nicky looked up and smiled shyly. "I like bacon."

Robert Williams walked in, and Nicky jumped. I said, "It's okay, Nicky. Mr. Williams is having breakfast with us."

Robert said, "What is he doing here? Isn't he supposed to be in the nursey?"

"Well, about that, I fired your nanny."

Robert looked irritated and asked, "Why?"

"Because I wanted to have breakfast with him, and she told me I had no rights, and I showed her who the boss was. Do you object?"

"I bet Mrs. Conner wasn't too happy about that! She never lets him out of that room."

"And you let her get away with that. Are you just mean or stupid?"

"Pardon me. I know nothing of children, so it wasn't my concern. Anyway, it's her job."

"Not anymore. I fired her."

Robert looked at me, glaring. "You don't have the right to come into my home and take over and start firing people."

"I beg your pardon, but when I talked to the attorneys, they informed me that the house and care of Nicky is my right. Or am I mistaken?" I said, smiling even though I just wanted to hit him.

Robert looked up sharply. "You have every right to do what you want, but I've been here since our parents died, and no one could even find you, so I've been in charge up until now," Robert said angrily, and the room got so quiet that you could feel tension in the air.

I talked with Nicky while he ate, and then I excused ourselves and went to the kitchen where Margaret was. She said that she really liked my bike and that she had one when she was younger. She and her husband bought one each for their tenth-year anniversary. I told her that was so sweet, and I asked if they rode still, but she said Larry passed away with cancer about ten years ago. She said that he rode up to the time he got sick, and after he passed away, she sold both bikes. I asked her how long she worked for my dad, and she said she'd been here about six years and that my dad was a good man to work for. I asked about Nicky, and she said my dad loved Nicky very much, but after he passed away, the nanny hardly let him out of her sight.

I took Nicky up to my room and sat him down on the bed, and then I went to the nursery to get him some clothes. Mrs. Conner was there, and she asked where Nickolas was. I said, "He's in my room. I'm getting him some clothes and toys, and I'll find him a bedroom so that he can sleep like a big boy, not a baby."

"He's a sweet child but lonely. He needs to be taken care of. It's my job to do. Mr. Williams will not be pleased."

I smiled and said, "No more. Your services are no longer needed."

"I'm going to Mr. Williams, and he'll take care of everything."

I picked out a T-shirt, an underwear, and a pair of jeans, and I walked past her. I went and helped Nicky take a bath and get dressed. Trina came to see if I needed anything, but I told her we were fine.

Nicky was a bright boy. He knew his age and his birthday, and he talked nonstop. I took Nicky down to the kitchen and asked Margaret if she knew where Nicky's toys were, but she said she didn't know if he had any. She very seldom saw him, and usually, it was when Mrs. Conner took him out in the evening for ten minutes or so. Margaret offered Nicky a cookie, and I asked her to watch over him while I went to find Mr. Williams. Margaret said he was in the study.

"Mr. Williams, do you have a minute? I need to talk to you." I asked

"I have time. What do you need?" Robert asked, sounding bored.

"It's about the nanny," I said. "We have a problem, and we need to get it worked out."

"His nanny will take care of him. She will feed him and take care of him, and you don't have to do anything for him. He has his own nanny, a maid, and a caretaker, so he's fine. What more could a child want?" Robert said.

"A lot more. He needs to play, have fun, and be around people. I think he needs to be a child, and since that wasn't the case, I fired Mrs. Conner."

"Mrs. Conner won't like that. She believes he needs to be kept on a strict schedule, and I don't think she'll like you messing it up. Let me see if I can smooth over everything. If I have to, I'll give her a bonus so that she'll not have hurt feelings," Robert said sternly.

"Are you for real? She's a horrid old woman that has no business taking care of a child. She's not taking care of Nicky, but if you want her to take care of you, that's fine with me. I like to see you sleeping in a crib!" I stomped out and slammed the door.

I went back to the kitchen, boiling mad. I told Margaret, "He's a little boy. He's too young to be on a strict schedule, and he has no friends. It's just not right. Do you know Robert wanted to give her a bonus and keep her here? But I told him he was crazy. I'll take Nicky shopping for clothes and toys, and can you ask the housekeeper to find Nicky a regular bedroom with no crib? I'll be back in a few minutes." I went upstairs to get my purse. Then I came back down and asked Margaret, "Can I drive dad's car to go shopping?"

"Of course, you can. I'll call Charles to bring the car around." Margaret called Charles. He wanted to know which car, and I said, "Any car. As long as it has a car seat for Nicky."

Robert came in and announced, "We need to talk and get things straight."

"Okay, but after I'm done with Nicky. I'm taking him shopping, and when I get back and put him down for his nap, I'll find you then," I said, took Nicky, and left.

We went shopping, and I bought Nicky clothes and some LEGOs and cars, and then I took him to McDonald's for lunch and playtime.

We came back, and I asked Charles if he could put Nicky's clothes and toys in his new room. I took Nicky outside to play and brought him in for a snack. After eating his snack, he was yawning, so I took him up to my room for a nap.

I went looking for Robert so we could discuss things, and I found him reading in the library.

"Nicky's down for a nap. Do you have time to talk now?" I asked.

"Nicky? Are you kidding me? His name is Nicholas, not Nicky," Robert said.

"He's a little boy, and Nicholas is too big a name for him," I said. "And do you know he still sleeps in a crib?"

"Does that matter? He has a nanny to make those decisions," Robert replied.

"No, he doesn't. He has me to make those decisions. I fired his nanny. She's rude and thinks you're the boss, and she's wrong," I said deliberately.

"I have been the boss ever since our parents got killed. And where were you? Nowhere to be found. So I took over, and they respect me," Robert said angrily.

"Well, not anymore. I'm here, and I'm taking over where Nicky is concerned. If you want the house, money, and everything, you can have it, but I'm taking care of Nicky like my father wanted. And if you have a problem with that, then tough shit," I said. "Does the staff respect you, or are they just afraid of you?" I slammed the door as I left.

I went upstairs to check on Nicky, and he wasn't in my bed, so I went to his room across from mine, but he wasn't there either. I went to the nursey, and Mrs. Connor had put him in the crib. She was just smiling, so I turned to her and said, "You're fired. Get your things and get out now. And don't come back to my house for any reason."

Mrs. Conner looked shock and said, "I'll go and talk to Mr. Williams."

"Go right ahead, but you're still fired," I said as I picked Nicky up.

I took Nicky downstairs to the kitchen and asked Mrs. Margaret if she could fix Nicky milk and cookies. Mrs. Margaret said of course, and I held Nicky and cuddled and played with him until he drank all his milk and ate his cookies. Then he wanted to go outside to play. I took him out to play on the old swing set in the backyard. It needed to be painted, but for now, Nicky could swing and play. He played for a while, and then I brought Nicky inside for a drink.

Mrs. Margaret said, "He's adorable and so sweet. When he was a baby, your father would bring him down sometimes, and they would eat snacks. But since your father passed, I haven't seen this baby very often. I knew he was here, but I haven't really seen him until today, and he's grown so much."

"Did you know Mrs. Conner had him sleeping in his crib still? He's almost four and too big for that crib. And by the way, I fired her. I'm sure there will be other problems." Mrs. Margaret laughed and said that she thought I could handle myself, and we both laughed. I took Nicky upstairs for a quick bath, dressed him in clean clothes, and then brought him down for dinner. Robert didn't show up for dinner even though he had his place on the table set. After dinner, I took Nicky out in the backyard again where the old swing set was. The swing set was metal and had a lot of rust on it. I remember when Momma had gotten me the swing set for my fifth birthday. I spent a lot of time out on it, and I remember it was red and white. Looking at it now, I really wanted it painted so Nicky could enjoy it like I did. It was still in good shape and very sturdy for its age. We played on the swing until dark. When I took Nicky inside for snacks, Robert was standing in the doorway, watching us and looking unhappy, so I smiled at him and winked and went into the kitchen. When we came back into the living room, Robert said, "Now that you're done playing mommy, can we talk seriously?"

"Sure. Let me run upstairs and get Nicky some toys to play with while we talk," I said.

"There are no toys here for Nicholas to play with. Mrs. Conner didn't approve of them, so she got rid of them after the funeral."

"How could she be so heartless? Children need stimulation. She's not a nanny. She's a nut," I said plainly. "I bought him a few toys earlier when we went out. I'll be right back."

Robert even cracked a smile over that remark, but it disappeared quickly. Then he cleared his throat and said, "I told her to take off a couple of days until things settled down."

I was outraged. "You told her what? I fired her, and she's not coming near Nicky ever again. And when I meet with the lawyer tomorrow and find out everything in the will, then we'll discuss if I can get a nanny for Nicky, but it won't be her." I picked up Nicky and walked out.

I went to find Charles and asked if there was a car that I could use while I was here, and he said there were several cars to choose from. He walked out with me to the garage, and there were five cars. I asked him why they needed five cars for two people, and he smiled and said Lady Chambers liked to drive different cars as much as possible. He showed me Dad's car, and it had a car seat. He showed me a dark-blue Cadillac sedan, and he showed me where all the keys were. I asked him whose car it was that I drove today, and he said it was the spare car for the nanny to use. I got Dad's keys and thanked him, and he smiled and said that I had my father's smile and that my dad was a good man. I didn't know what to say because my dad wasn't a good father when I was growing up, but I guess he did his best after my mom passed away. Although when he met Clair Hudson, everything got exceedingly worse. After I got Nicky and settled him into his room with his twin bed, he asked if he could have the bear he got when we went shopping, so I gave it to him, tucked him in, and kissed him good night. Then Trina read him a story, and he went right to sleep.

I got up early and checked on Nicky who was still asleep, so I showered, changed into a pink sundress, and went downstairs for coffee. Trina came in with Nicky twenty minutes later, and I helped Nicky with his plate. He ate really well, and then I took him upstairs, washed him up, and changed his clothes. I took my purse, and we went to the garage to leave, but Robert was there, looking at us angrily. He asked where we were going, and I told him that it was none of his business but that we wouldn't be out too long. I put Nicky in his car seat and buckled him in, and I ignored Robert who was standing there and watching us. I got inside the car, and we left. I could see Robert in the rearview mirror, and he looked livid, which just made me feel better. I took Nicky shopping and bought him toys, not a lot but something he could play indoors and some for outdoors. Nicky picked out a dark-brown teddy bear and asked if he could have it, and I said of course he could. Then we stopped for lunch and ice cream. Nicky felt sleepy on the way home, so I carried him in and took him upstairs to his room. Trina came in, and she and Charles brought our bags in. She offered to move me to the nursery and told me the adjoining room could be turned into Nicky's room, but I told her that Nicky already liked his room.

Charles and Todd, the handyman, unloaded the car and brought everything upstairs. Nicky had woken up and was climbing in and out of his bed. He asked if he could have his stuffed bear to sleep with, so I gave it to him. Then I took him down for dinner. Robert was at the table, and he smiled and asked if we had a good day.

I said, "Yes. I took him shopping for clothes and toys, and he had a good day. He has really good manners for a three-year-old."

"I bet Mommy dearest made sure he did," Robert replied.

After dinner, Trina took Nicky upstairs, bathed him, and put him in his pajamas. He looked so cute and was so happy smiling and talking and was telling Trina about McDonald's. There was a movement behind me, and Robert was standing there, watching. He had a look on his face as if amazed at watching Nicky play. I gave Nicky a good night kiss and asked Trina to read a story to him. I smiled at Robert and went downstairs to the kitchen, and he followed behind. I was afraid of another confrontation, but instead, Robert said, "I've never seen such a happy kid. Before you came, I don't think I had ever seen him smile or play or get excited about a bed and a bear."

"He's a little boy full of energy and excitement. And really, can you imagine any child getting excited over Mrs. Conner?" I said, smiling.

Robert smiled and almost laughed. "I see your point on Mrs. Conner. I'll call her tomorrow and tell her that she's not needed, okay? Can we call a truce and try to work together until we get this all figured out?"

"Yes, a truce it is! Would you like some hot tea or coffee? I'm in the mood for hot tea and cake, so I hope I can find some," I said, looking in the cabinets. "Yes, I found tea. And Mrs. Margaret made a lemon cake today. Join me?"

"Sure, but I'll have coffee with my cake," Robert said.

We talked for over an hour, and I asked him about how he felt about his mother marrying my father. He said, "It made no difference to me. I was sent to boarding school after Clair married my dad, and I didn't come home very much. I was seven when my dad died of a heart attack, and Clair didn't even inform me of my father's death until after the funeral."

"That's terrible! Why would your mother do that to you?"

"My mother died of cancer when I was six, and Clair was her nurse. Within months of Mom's passing, they got married, and I was shipped to a boarding school in the second grade."

"How could your dad let that happen to you? You were just a child."

"Clair ran everything where my father was concerned. During the summer months, I went to my grandparents' house, and Dad might come see me once, and I never came home for the holidays as I got older. My grandparents passed away, so I spent most of the summer and holidays with my friends and their families. When my dad died of a heart attack and left everything to me in the will, Clair called and started playing the concerned stepmother because my father left everything to me, except the house and a small allowance, so she would call me if she needed money. I kept her on a tight leash, so that's why she married your dad: because he had money. I'm surprised you weren't sent to boarding school."

"I was in high school, but she made my life hell. I couldn't get a high school ring unless I worked and paid for it, and Dad gave me a car, but she wanted me to buy it, so I got a job and walked and caught buses to work and saved my money. They didn't come to my graduation because she had made lunch plans and it would be rude to cancel, and my dad let her run things. After I graduated, I stayed with a friend for a few months and worked. Then one day, I took all my money and bought my first Harley and packed what I needed and left. I haven't been back until I got the letter from the lawyer, and here I am.

"What I can't understand is why they had Nicky. My dad wasn't a great father. He tried, but after Mom passed away, he just left me to myself. Then he came home one afternoon and had Clair with him and announced that they got married. Neither one showed any affection to me, so why become parents again?" I asked.

Robert said that he didn't know but that we would find out tomorrow how the accident happened. I rinsed the dishes off and put them in the sink and said good night to Robert. I went to check on Nicky and went to bed. I slept nicely. I got up early and checked on Nicky who was still asleep. I showered and dressed in a light-blue floral dress and went downstairs for coffee. Mrs. Margaret was cooking breakfast and had coffee ready, and she told me I looked nice. She asked if I was nervous about meeting the lawyers, but I assured her I was fine and said, "I hope you didn't mind, but we had coffee and cake last night."

Mrs. Margaret said, "That was fine, but you didn't have to clean up. I would have done it when I got here."

I told her about taking Nicky to McDonald's for dinner and shopping and how things seemed to be better between me and Robert since he agreed that Mrs. Conner was done and not coming back. She said she was glad; that woman had no sense when it came to children. Trina brought Nicky down and bathed and dressed him in play clothes. She offered to feed him, but I said he could eat at the table with me. I needed to get a booster seat so he could reach the table, and Trina said there was one in the basement that the nanny sent down, so she went and got it. Mrs. Margaret wiped it down, and I buckled him in it and gave him a plate with scrambled eggs, sausage, and toast, and he was eating when Robert came in.

Nicky looked up, and Robert said, "Good morning. Did you sleep nicely? I didn't realize it was so late until I went to my room." Then he smiled and said, "Hello, Nicky." Nicky looked up, smiled, and said, "Hi," and then he continued to eat. Robert said, "Do all little boys make mess when eating?"

"Yes, especially when they start learning, and I think he's enjoying learning, don't you?" I said, smiling, and Robert laughed. Just then, I realized how handsome he was. He had dark-brown eyes and a great smile. I thought to myself, Oh no, I'm not going to fall for him. He's too unpredictable, and I don't need that kind of complication now that I had to think about Nicky first. Trina and Mrs. Margaret took care of Nicky while we went to the study room when the lawyers came for our meeting.

The lawyers introduced themselves as Mr. Krieg and Mr. Townson, attorneys at law. They asked if Mr. Black was coming to the meeting, but I said no. He was in Texas, but if I needed him, all I had to do was call. Robert looked surprise about my lawyer but didn't say anything. They read off the will in more detail than they had sent to George, but everything was left to me and Nicky. There were two houses and an island that Dad had bought two years ago, and there was a lot of money left to me and a trust fund for Nicky. They went over everything, and it took almost two hours. Afterward, they gave me two letters and a DVD for me and Nicky. Then Mr. Krieg wanted to read the accident reports and medical findings for the autopsies.

The findings were conclusive that Clair was driving with a blood alcohol content above the limit and that my father had no alcohol but he had an extremely high dose of rat poison. It appeared that it was ingested over a period of months and that he bled out because of the accident. The county attorneys were looking into several deaths similar to this, and they said that Clair Chambers was associated with them, including her previous husbands. A total of four husbands who had no previous medical concerns all died, as well as several of her patients when she worked for hospice. The county attorney would get in touch with us if they find anything. They expressed their condolences and left. I was in shock and asked Robert if he knew about this, and he said that after the accident, the police asked him questions concerning his mother, thinking Clair was his mother. He explained to them that she wasn't his biological mother and that his mother got sick and Clair was the hospice nurse that took care of her. They asked if they could exhume his mother's body, and he gave permission. Then they asked for permission for his father's body, so he suspected something, but he didn't know what happened until today. After the lawyers left, I called George and told him what had come out in the meeting, and he said that when he talked with one of the attorneys, he mentioned that there was a chance of foul play. We talked for thirty minutes, and I told him I'd call him on Sunday and check on him. After I got off the phone, I went and got Nicky and took him outside to play. We were on the swing when Robert came out and asked if I was okay. He sat on the swing with me, and when Nicky climbed into his lap, Robert looked terrified.

"He's just a little boy. He won't hurt you," I told him.

Robert smiled and said, "I don't want to hurt him. I've never been around kids. I've never even held a baby or a little one before."

I explained, "Nicky must like you and feel safe, or he wouldn't have climbed into your lap." We sat on the swing, playing with Nicky. Robert seemed to get more comfortable with him.

Then Robert asked, "Would you like to go out for dinner and relax after the day we've had?"

I accepted, and Trina took care of Nicky. Robert suggested Longhorn, so before we left, I asked if I could drive, and he said sure if that was what I wanted.

I changed into jeans and a dressy T-shirt, and he wore jeans and a button-down shirt. When we went to leave, I went to my Harley, and Robert stopped dead in his tracks and said, "I thought you wanted to drive the car."

I smiled and said, "No. I want to take Harley out."

"You name your motorcycle?" Robert asked.

"No. It's a Harley Davidson. I just want to get out and feel free. It will do you some good also. Or are you chickening out?"

"No Melissa, I'm not chickening out, but I haven't been on a motorcycle in years."

"Robert, can you call me Missy? That's what everyone calls me. Even Charles and Trina does."

"If employees get too familiar, then it's hard to demand respect," Robert said.

"You're too uptight. You need to relax and enjoy life and take it one day at a time. Now are you coming or not?" I asked him, laughing

"Okay, but I'm not uptight," Robert said as he climbed on the bike. We drove down through the park and over the bridge to the lake, and we rode around town before getting dinner. I had a good time, and so did

Robert, it seemed. After dinner, we drove around town again, and then we went home.

As I got off the bike, I turned and asked Robert if he had a good time. He caught my hand, pulled me close, and kissed me. It was a long, deep kiss that stirred things that I hadn't thought about for a long time. I pulled back and smiled, and I said it's late and I needed to check on Nicky and get some sleep. I ran upstairs and looked at Nicky who was sleeping soundly. I went and stripped off, put on a light night gown, and lay in bed thinking about the kiss and reminisced. John was my boyfriend when I first moved to Texas, and I thought we had a future, but then he got hit by a semi and never woke up. We had only dated a few months and spent one weekend together. It was magic; he was so gentle because it was my first time, and we had a great weekend. We had plans on going to Alabama the next weekend to meet his parents, but that weekend never came. I did meet his parents at the funeral home, and they said he was so excited for them to meet me. We kept in touch for a while, but then as time went by, we lost contact.

I got up and went downstairs for a cup of hot tea. It was so late at night, so I didn't put on a robe.

The house was quiet. I fixed my tea and sliced a piece of cake, and then the light came on. It was Robert. "Sorry, I heard something. I'll let you be," he said, and he turned to leave, but he stopped and turned around. "I'm sorry about earlier. I didn't mean to offend you. I just got caught up in the moment."

"You didn't offend me. It's just been a long time since I got kissed and felt something, and it scared me." I told him.

"You don't have to be afraid. I would never hurt you. I'm not sure what this is, but I feel something for you that I have never felt before," Robert said quietly.

"I know what you mean, but I have to consider everything now. What I do will effect Nicky, and he has to be my priority first and foremost. I hope you understand."

"Yes, I understand. But maybe we can explore what this is between us and what it means in our lives with each other and Nicky. After all, he's my family too." Robert said with a small smile and desire in his eyes.

"Okay, but we'll take it slow, all right?" I asked.

Robert smiled and walked over and kissed me gently at first and then more intense before pulling back and saying, "Good night." He then walked out of the kitchen. I just stood there, shaken with desire. I took my tea and the cake up to my room.

I had a rough night. I dreamed about John and Robert, so when I got up, it was later than usual, and I had a headache. I showered, got dressed, and went downstairs. Trina had Nicky eating, and Robert was at the table drinking coffee and looking like he was playing with his food.

"Hello. Beautiful morning," I said, acting like nothing had happened.

There was a knock on the door, and Charles came in and said the police was there to speak with us. Trina kept Nicky, and we went to the library to meet with the police. A young man, probably in his early thirties, introduced himself. "Hello. I'm Detective Jones, and I'm following up on your parents' accident."

"Nice to meet you, but she wasn't my parent. My dad married her shortly after my mom passed away," I said. Detective Jones went over some basic information and asked, "When was the last time you saw or spoke to your father?"

"I hadn't talked or seen my father for about six years now," I replied.

"What about you, Mr. Williams? When was the last time you saw or talked with your mother?"

"She wasn't my mother. She was my stepmom, and she sent me to a boarding school until my father passed away. As I was in control of my father's money, she clung to me as if I was her child," Robert said. "I haven't seen Clair or Jonathon in almost a year."

"When was the last time you talked to her?" Detective Jones asked.

"About six months ago, she called and asked if I still had the condo in the Islands, but I told her I had sold it." Robert replied.

"Did she say why she wanted to know?"

"No. She said okay and hung up."

"Thank you for answering my questions. After we get all the facts, we'll be in touch," said Detective Jones, and Robert walked him to the door.

I had a headache starting, so I went to see if I could get coffee. Margaret was in the kitchen putting food away. When she saw me, she smiled and handed me a fresh cup of coffee and a plate of blueberry scones. "Thanks," I said.

Trina had taken Nicky up for a bath and to play with him, so I hung out with Margaret in the kitchen. Margaret asked me about my life and if I had someone special.

I said, "No. I don't have time for anyone but George and now Nicky. I just hope I figure out how to take care of Nicky and not screw it up."

"You'll do fine. You're like your father; he had a big heart, and I can tell that you do too, just from the way you talk about your George," Margaret said.

"It's hard to believe that everyone thinks my dad was great but me. After he married Clair, my life was hell, and he never had a moment for me, and Clair was just mean to me. I can't understand why they had Nicky."

"People do strange things for love. It doesn't matter if it's between a man and woman or father and daughter or just two friends. Sometimes, people do things that they think are the best for the one they love, even if it doesn't seem like it."

"You could be right, but for now, I'm going to call George and check on him. And if Trina is taking a good care of Nicky, I'm taking Tylenol and maybe a nap for a while," I said as I walked out of the kitchen.

I called George, and when we were talking, he asked me about Robert Williams. I said, "He's the uncle. He's Clair's stepson, and he has been here taking care of everything until I was informed. Why?"

George said, "Well, I just got off the phone with him, and he was asking our relationship and wanted to know about you and if you had someone special in your life besides me. I told him that anything he wanted to know about you, he needs to ask you."

I was so mad at Robert. He had no right to call George. My life was none of his business. I'm not playing games when it comes to George; he's been nothing but a friend, more like a dad to me.

"Thank you, George. You're the best. I'll call you and check on you later tonight. Love you," I said and hung up.

I then went looking for Robert, but I could not find him.

I lay down after taking Tylenol, and Trina and Mrs. Margaret took care of Nicky. I got up for dinner but didn't eat much. I played with Nicky until bedtime, and then I went to my room and called George to check on him. He sounded tired and concerned about me, but I assured George that everything was fine and told him to get some rest. Then I called Shelly and asked her to check on George for me and spend some extra time with him and to call me if there were any concerns.

I went looking for Robert. I found him in the library, reading. When I entered, he looked up.

"How dare you call George and ask questions about my relationship with him? You have no right! I am done with this crap. I'm making arrangements for me and Nicky to fly home tomorrow, and we won't be back." I slammed the door and went to my room. I called the airline and booked seats for 11:00 a.m. tomorrow, and then I called detective Jones and told him that I was going home and that if they needed me, they could find me in Texas. They had my address and information.

Detective Jones said that once the investigation was done, he would call me and let me know the details. I thanked him, and after I got off the phone, I called George and let him know I was coming home tomorrow. I packed mine and Nicky's clothes, and then I went to bed. Robert knocked on my door several times, but I didn't answer. I just wanted to go home. I got up early, showered, and dressed in black pants and a white blouse, and I had Trina to take Nicky down to breakfast. I wrote several notes to Mrs. Margaret, Charles, Trina, and also one to Robert. I thanked them for welcoming me and being so nice and helpful but that we were heading home. I gave each one a $2,500 check. I explained that Robert would handle everything and that this is a bonus and that they deserved it. I gave them my number and address and asked them to keep in touch. I asked Mrs. Margaret to watch over my Harley, and maybe I'll be back one day.

Roberts's letter looked like this:

Robert

Thank you for everything you've done, but since you don't trust me and my word, we have nothing between us. I wish you well, and please handle the house and employees, and just relax and have fun sometimes. I wish you happiness.

Missy

Then I asked Charles to take me and Nicky to the airport, and we flew home. When we arrived in Texas, we stayed the night in Galantine, and then the next day, I rented a car and drove home. I called George and told him we'd see him the next day. I wanted him to meet Nicky.

When we got in, I unloaded the car and went to check on Sally. She was glad I came home, and she played with Nicky and gave him milk and homemade cookies. I called Shelly and asked if she could take me to turn in the rental car, and she said she would be there in an hour. After dropping the car off, I suggested we stop for dinner and she could catch me up on what I missed. We went to Ponderosa, and I got Nicky and my plate while Shelly watched him, and then she got hers. I took Sally to the doctor one day, and we dropped by to check on George. He asked us to stay for lunch, so I went and got subway, and when I got back, they were both blushing. After that Sally, rode over with me several times. She even stayed the weekend with George because I was supposed to get Ruthie to check on them but her mom needed her that weekend, so Sally said she and George would be fine together. After we ate, Shelly took us home, and I told her to keep the car until morning. I said I'd call her when I needed the car and that I had plans to sleep in and then go see George around lunchtime.

I got Nicky settled in, and we went to visit Sally and brought Tabby home. We played with Tabby until it was late, and then I put Nicky in my bed, and he asked if Tabby could sleep with him. I said yes, and he slept all night and got up after nine that morning. I fixed him a breakfast bowl since I hadn't been to the store for groceries. I made a list for the grocery and a list for Nicky, like clothes, toys, and snacks. I called Shelly, and she said she would be there around noon, so I bathed Nicky and got him dressed. I aired the apartment out since I wasn't home for a few weeks, and it smelled musky. Shelly arrived a few minutes before noon, and I had called George and told him I'd be over around one and that I'd bring lunch. I paid Shelly and dropped her off at her mom's house. We went to Subway and got lunch and then drove to George's house.

It was good to see George. I hugged him and introduced Nicky to him. George was excited to meet Nicky. They talked and played, and George asked me to go into the blue bedroom and get some toys for Nicky to play with. I had never been in the blue bedroom because it was his son's room. His son was in his early twenties when he got killed, so I was surprised that George would have toys from James's childhood, but he did. I brought out cars and trucks for Nicky to play with, and I got to talk to George. He looked tired, and I felt like something was going on with him. After they ate, Nicky played himself into a nap while holding a police car. George told me to lay him on the couch, so I did. Then I asked, "George, it's so good to be home, but you look tired. What did the doctor say when you went last week?"

George smiled and said, "You worry too much. I'm fine."

"I worry about you. Now what did Dr. Rogers say?"

"I canceled my appointment. I was worried about you in case I needed to fly out, but now that you're back, I'll reschedule. I promise," George said, smiling.

"I'll call now and get your appointment. You look tired and pale, and I need to know that you're doing okay," I said. I got up and called the doctor's office. I got off the phone and came in and sat by George. I smiled and said, "The nurse asked if you are ready to make the appointment with Dr.

Craig, and I told her yes, you are ready and that I'd be taking you, and she gave me all the information."

George looked like he got caught with his hand in the cookie jar. He said, "I planned on telling you, but I didn't want to worry you with everything going on."

"George, no matter what's going on, you're my priory next to Nicky. You're all I have, and you mean the world to me. You can always count on me. That's what's family for, and you're my family." I got up and hugged him. "We'll get through this, and don't ever be afraid of telling me anything. Got it?" I said.

Nicky woke up and started playing again, and we stayed all afternoon. Then I took him to the grocery, and we got everything I could think of that little boys eat. I picked up groceries for George and stopped by and got his medicine at the pharmacy. The pharmacist asked if I had any questions about his new medication, and I asked what it was for, and she said it helped with the side effects of chemo and that he needed to take it at least two weeks before starting chemo. I told her I would make sure he did and thanked her. We got George a pepperoni pizza for his dinner, and I took Nicky in to play while I unloaded the car. I took the pizza and medicine in last, and after putting George's groceries away, I sat beside him and asked, "How long have you known about the cancer? I picked up your medicine, and the pharmacist said not to start it until two weeks before you start chemo."

George said, "I found out the day after you left. I had a spell, and Shelly took me to the hospital. They kept me overnight and ran tests and found lung cancer, so I went to my doctor, and he wants me to see Dr. Craig and start chemo as soon as possible. That's who I had an appointment with that I canceled last week. I just didn't want to worry you. I am sorry. I'll call tomorrow and reschedule."

"When I called the doctor, they called me back with your appointment for Friday at one, and I'm taking you." I said.

"You have little Nicky, so I'll call a taxi."

"I'll get Shelly to watch Nicky, okay? I'm here for you. Whenever you need me, I'm here."

"I don't want to be a burden on you. You have Nicky to take care of. You don't need an old sick man to also take care of," George said.

"George, you're a nut. I love you. You're the only family I have, and I plan on helping you beat this. We're a team and always will be okay," I said.

I got George settled down after dinner, and then I took Nicky home. We played for a while, and then I washed Nicky and put him in his pajamas. I put him in bed and read him a story, and he was asleep before I got halfway through The Three Little Pigs. Sally called and asked if she could come over, and I said yes and that I would love the company. I started tea, and Sally was at the door with an orange spice cake, so we snacked, and Sally told me about George's health. I told her I knew and how I found out but that I would always be there for him and her also, but then she told me her son wants her to move in with him and his family. They live in Alabama, and they want to spend as much time with her so that she could get to know his children before something happens. His wife's mother just passed from a heart attack, and it made them realized how fragile life is. Thus, Sally planned on moving on September. We talked until it was late, and after Sally left, I realized that I wouldn't have anyone here in these apartments. I knew almost nobody, and everyone was new except Sally and me. I went to bed with a heavy heart, knowing George was sick and Sally was moving.

I had a restless night, and I got up, cleaned the house, and was almost done when Nicky came into the kitchen. After giving him hugs and kisses, I fixed him cereal, and I finished the dishes while he ate. He was such a good boy; he never seemed to get upset or cry and never complained.

After he finished his cereal, I got a call from Detective Jones. He informed me that there was a private investigator that Clair Chambers had hired to find me, because she knew that my father had changed his will and was leaving everything to me. That was probably why she was poisoning him. After I got off the phone, I gave Nicky a bath, dressed him in his play clothes, and then took him to the park down the street. He played in the sand, swing, and climbed the monkey bars. He was afraid of the slide, so I climbed up and put him in my lap, and down we went. He laughed and giggled and said, "Let's do it again," and so we did several times.

Then I told him we would come back another time and play. We went home, and I wiped him down, changed his clothes, and took him shopping. I bought him clothes, toys, and got him to ride on the arcade police car. It had bells, whistles, and lights. After checking out, we went to get fish and fries for lunch and rode to George's house.

George was lying down, but he got up when we got there. After lunch, he asked if I could take him to the DMV to pay his taxes and get his tags. I told him I could do it myself, but he said he wanted to get out. We took him, and he asked if I could walk in with him. I and Nicky sat in the first roll, and they called George's number. I helped him up to the counter and sat back down, but George called for me to come up and sign a paper, and I did, but no one said what I was signing. Then George asked if I could walk him over to the courthouse, and we did, and then he signed papers and had me sign also. I did, and I wanted to ask what I was signing. He always told me to read everything before signing anything, but when it came to George, I trust him completely. We came out of the courthouse, I asked George why I needed to sign, and he told me that he gave me power of attorney over his health and over his estate. I told him he needed to find someone smarter than me because I didn't even know what I was signing, but he told me he wanted me to have everything in case something happened to him. I decided to wait until we were back at the house to discuss this.

We stopped at Subway for dinner, and then we went home. I fixed George's and Nicky's plate, and while Nicky ate and watched TV, I decided it was time to talk to George about his health and me being given his power of attorney. I looked at George and realized how bad he looked and how I never noticed him feeling under the weather before, let alone having cancer. That was such a scary word, and here was George facing it. I didn't know what to say. I smiled and moved over to sit beside George and said, "George, I love you, and I'll be here and help you, but I don't know about being your power of attorney, don't you think you need someone that knows what to do?"

George looked up from his sandwich and smiled and said, "I want you to have all of this. My house, my car, and my money. No one ever does anything just out of kindness of their heart except you. You stayed with me through the worst time of my life, and you made me want to go on after I lost Sophie. You took care of me, and you've been taking care of me ever since. I really appreciated it, and you won't take my money not even for lunch. You're such a special lady, and I wish I had a daughter like you, and since I don't, and I love you like a daughter, I want you to have everything. Everything I have is paid off, and it belongs to you now."

I laughed. "We make a good pair, don't we? You lost your son and wife, and I never had a family that gave a damn about me, so I think we make a great family, and you don't have to worry. I'll take great care of you, and we'll beat this cancer." I hugged George.

He then said, "I plan on going into the hospice hospital. I don't want to be a burden on you, and besides, you have Nicky now. You don't have time to play nurse to a sick old man"

"The hell you will. I plan on taking care of you. I'd never put you in a place like that. We'll go to see your doctor, and he'll have your treatment all planned out. I don't want to hear you talk like that. George, I can't lose you. You're all I have," I said, almost in tears.

"You have your whole life to plan out for you and Nicky, and you don't need to bother with me. I'll be fine at the hospital," George said.

"I'm going with you to your doctor's appointment, and then we'll discuss this, okay?" I said through tears

"Now don't cry. What will Nicky think? Let's finish our dinner, and then I'm going to lie down and rest," he said.

I picked at my food instead of eating it. I lost my appetite, so I cleaned up and straightened the kitchen up, while George and Nicky watched cartoons. Then I asked George if he needed anything before we left, and he said no. I got Nicky ready, and George handed me keys. I guess I looked dumbfounded, and George said, "Here are the keys to the house, my car, and my truck. I paid the insurance on them both for a year, and the homeowner's insurance I paid last month for a year before I found out about my health."

"I can't take your keys. This is your house and autos," I said.

"Come here, and sit down, Missy. I have something to show you." He walked over to his desk and sat in his favorite chair. I thought that the chair needed to be replaced, but George loved it so; it was the last gift that Sophie had given him. I went and sat down, and George got some papers out of his desk and handed them to me. It was his will. I handed it back to him, but he said, "I want you to read it, and I want you to look at the date." It was prepared and notarized. I read the document and looked at the dates, and it was written two years ago. I looked shocked and said, "Have you been sick this long?" and George said, "No, but I knew my wishes back then. I love you like my daughter, and I'm very proud of you. So you see, me getting cancer didn't change a thing. I want you to have this house and all of my things, and if you want to sell them, then I'm fine with that. I just want you to be happy. This is my gift to you because I think of you as my family."

I went over to George and hugged him and said, "Thank you, but what about giving them to your favorite charity?"

George smiled and said, "You are my favorite charity, and I don't want to hear anything else about my will, okay? The papers you signed today was me putting your name on all of my property and cars, and tomorrow, we'll go to the bank, and I'll put you on my accounts. Come on, give me a hug, and take Nicky home. It's getting late."

On the way home, we stopped at McDonald's for chicken nuggets for Nicky. After eating, I bathed him and put him in his pajamas, and we watched cartoons until his bedtime. Then I put him down and went to watch the news. The weatherman said that Pennsylvania was having torrential rain and storms with flooding, hail, and massive power outages, including Garrettsville outside of Pittsburg where Robert, Margaret, and everybody was back home. I called the house and got the message that "All circuits were busy, please try your call later," so I called Robert's cell phone, and he answered. "Robert, it's me Missy. I just saw the weather report. How's everything back home?"

Robert said stiffly, "It's fine. Just some rain and lightning. Nothing serious. No reason to concern you with."

"Okay, sorry, I called. I was just worried. I won't bother you again." I hung up, aggravated. Why act that way? He was the one who didn't trust me, and that was all on him. I got up and went to bed. I dreamed bad dreams all night, so I got up with a headache.

I fixed pancakes and bacon for breakfast; Nicky loved pancakes. Then I got him cleaned up for the day, and while he watched cartoons, I took a quick shower and got dressed. I fixed pancakes and bacon for George, and as we left to see him, Sally caught me and asked about George. She knew about his cancer, and they had developed a friendship. Sally said she was going to miss him when she leaves, which was moved up to June six weeks from now. Her son was coming to get her then, so she asked if I had any time and if I could help her pack, and I told her I would. I told her I would call Shelly and have her help also. Then we went to George's house. When we got there, his neighbor Matt was knocking on the door, and I asked if something was the matter. He said George fell on the porch last night, and he just wanted to make sure he was okay, so I used the keys George gave me to let myself in.

I yelled for George, and I found him on his couch, lying there in pain. His head had dry blood on his forehead, and his arm was bleeding. He was trying to get up, but he couldn't, so I grabbed a wash cloth and cleaned him up while Matt called an ambulance. Rachel, Matt's wife, came over and took Nicky so he wouldn't be scared of the sirens. The EMTs checked on George and said he needed to go to the hospital for x-rays. Matt and Rachel offered to keep Nicky; they had their grandkids today, and they were close to his age, so I went with George to the hospital.

He was lucky; the doctor said he had not broken anything, but he had a concussion, and since he was at the hospital, they had to keep him overnight for observation. I stayed with him most of the day, and then he told me to go get Nicky and go home. He said he was fine, and the nurse said the doctors would be in early morning. George's cancer doctor said he would be here around lunchtime, so I took Nicky home. While he played, we ate an early dinner, and then I called Margaret. I asked about the weather, and she said they were lucky that they had no damage and flooding in their area. We talked for about ten minutes. I asked about everybody, and she said Robert left the house over two weeks ago, and she didn't know where he went, but everybody else was doing great. After I got off the phone, I wondered where Robert was. I thought it didn't matter to me, but it did, and I just didn't want to admit it. I got up early and had Sally watch over Nicky. Shelly was coming over around nine so they could start packing and watch Nicky while I went to the hospital. I checked with the nurse to see how George did last night, and she said he slept well and that the doctors are making their rounds now, so I went to see George. He was sleeping, but you could tell he was feeling pain, so I woke him up and asked him if he needed anything. He said no, but he was glad I was there so he could leave. I helped him wash his face and brush his teeth, and then the doctor came in and said that he had a slight concussion but nothing broken and that the cancer doctor was on his way in. The doctor said he was lucky and that he had a great daughter to help take care of him. He said it's hard today to find adult children willing to help their parents and that George was very lucky. George told the doctor he was very lucky indeed and very proud of his daughter. Then after the doctor left, we laughed about it.

The cancer doctor came in, and everything went downhill from there. Dr. Scott came in and asked me to have a seat. It was time to honestly talk about cancer and George's options. Dr. Scott said, "Mr. Black, I have all your test back, and it's time to face the reality of what you're in for."

George said, "I know how serious it is, and I've made all my final arrangements."

"We need to discuss chemo and radiation treatment," Dr. Scott said.

"No, we don't. You told me there was nothing that could be done, so I'm not spending my final days sick and in pain. I've made up my mind. I have Missy to help me, and when it gets to be bad, I'll check in at the hospice."

"But with chemo and radiation, you could live another six months, or maybe even a year. Without treatment, you're looking at maybe three to four months. I know your daughter wants you for longer than that."

"Doctor, I'm old, tired, and sick. I'm ready to go home and be with my Sophie. She's in heaven waiting for me. I've made up my mind, and I'm not changing it," George said.

"Okay, if that's what you want, I will give you meds to help with the pain and sickness until you need hospice. I truly wish I had better news, but I'm glad you have such a good daughter that loves you so much and will help you and be there. I'll check in on you before you go home this afternoon." And with that, Dr. Scott left.

We left in the late afternoon, and I got George home and settled in. I called Shelly to check on Nicky and Sally, and she said they were fine and that they were on the way to Subway, and then they would be over. They brought George his favorite sub, and Sally visited with George, while Shelly and I talked. She had Sally all packed up, except for what she needs on a daily basis and that she would help her again on the date closer to her leaving. Shelly called goodwill to come and pick up what she didn't keep, and she talked with Sally's son. They were coming in a few weeks to get her. I told her about George's health and that me and Nicky would be moving in to help take care of him. After dinner, Shelly took Sally home and said she would leave my car keys with Sally, but I told her to keep them. I was giving her my car, and it could be a while before I could get it transferred, but I had insurance on it, and she was covered until we change the title. Shelly gave me a big hug and thanked me. Then she offered to help out with Nicky and George anytime. After they left, I checked on George who was watching TV, so I gave Nicky his bath and got him in his pajamas and took him down to tell George good night. George flipped over to cartoons, and he and Nicky watched cartoons for thirty minutes. Then I put Nicky down for the night, and I helped George get ready for bed. After I got everyone down for the night, I called Margaret back and checked on everyone down home. Everything was good; Robert had left and set up payroll with the housekeeper, and Margaret had control over the household bills, and everything was good. She asked if I was coming home, but I told her about George and that I would come maybe in the fall. I said I would call and check on things again and that she could call anytime also. I slept well that night, but I dreamed about Robert, which happened these days more often than not. I got up; Nicky was still sleeping, so I fixed breakfast and coffee, and then I went and checked on George. He was just getting up, so I helped him wash up and got his clothes for him, and while he got dressed, I put breakfast on. Nicky came downstairs and said he wanted bacon, which is his favorite, so I fixed bacon and scrambled eggs on his plate. Then George came to the table, so I helped him with his plate too. We had a good breakfast, and then George took Nicky and went to watch TV while I cleaned up.

George wanted to go run errands, so we went to church, and he talked with the priest about his health and what he wanted. Then I took him to the funeral home and went shopping for a new suit, and George bought Nicky clothes and toys. He also bought several things that he wouldn't tell me about. We had a late lunch at the Boesky's Bar and Grille. George's order was bacon cheeseburger, and he ate some of it, but then he looked so tired, so I had the waitress bag up our food, and I took George home. I insisted he take a nap and he agreed, which was unusual, but I didn't say anything. I also noticed he took his pain medicine before lying down.

Over the next several days, I had Shelly help me move mine and Nicky's things to George's house. I gave most of my furniture to Shelly, her mom, and her sister. I packed up anything that I wanted and put them in storage in George's garage. We got settled in and said our goodbyes to Sally at dinner at Giorgio's Italian restaurant Friday evening. Shelly met us there after she picked up Sally, and me and George brought Nicky and got there early and ordered a cake for her to celebrate her birthday on Monday since she wouldn't be here.

Everybody had a good time. We're going to miss Sally. She was the first person I met when I moved to Texas, and she was there for me anytime I needed her. She got me through losing John, and she tried to get me to go out and find love, but I wasn't ready; and now, she's leaving, and it's like losing another family member. I know she's excited about moving in with her son; she's so proud of him and Casey, his wife, and they have three boys and a girl, and she couldn't wait to meet them all. I told her if she ever needed me, all she had to do was call. I gave Sally a diamond cross for her birthday from all of us, and she was touched that we thought that much of her; and I told her that she was the mom and that's what I thought of her and that I loved her and would dearly miss her. After hugs and tears, everybody went home. George was tired, so I helped him to bed and got his medicine for him. He looked up and said, "I'm sorry about being sick and weak and having you to take care of me."

"I wouldn't have it any other way, George. I love you, and I'm quite capable of taking care of you, and I want to. I can't stand the thought of you going to the hospital and be all alone," I said. I bent down and kissed George on his forehead and said, "Good night."

I helped Nicky change into his pajamas, and I read a story to him, and he fell asleep. I showered and put on a night gown and sat down. I was watching TV when my phone rang. "Hello?" I said. There was silence on the phone, but I could tell someone was there. As I started to hang up, Robert said, "Melissa, it's Robert. Do you have a few minutes to talk?" As if he could see me nod my head yes, I said, "Yes, of course. Can I help you? Is everything okay at home?"

He said, "Yes, everything's fine in Pennsylvania. What I need to talk to you about is the results of the investigation on Clair."

"Okay. I haven't heard anything, so I figured they didn't find anything."

Robert said the investigation found that Clair murdered all of her six husbands and at least fifteen people that she took care of in a hospice.

My head was spinning. "Did they have names on any of her clients that she killed?"

"If you're asking if she murdered your mom, they wouldn't tell me names," Robert said. "But the detective did say that he was contacting every victim's family members, and we would just have to wait. He couldn't tell me anything else yet."

"Did he say when he would be contacting people?" I asked.

Robert responded, "No. Just that we had to wait until they have all the facts, and then he would tell me, but I wanted you to know just in case you hear from him."

"Okay, thanks. I appreciate you calling me with the update."

"No problem. How's Nicky doing?"

"He's doing great. How about you? Are you still uptight or are you having fun yet?"

Robert laughed. "I'm still uptight, I guess, but I'm trying."

It was my turn to laugh. "You know what, life's too short. You need to just let go and do something you always wanted to do. Try something fun or an adventure. Do something you've always wanted to. Do go travel somewhere, or, hell, buy a boat and go boating. Please don't put off something thinking later would be better because you may not have later. We're not promised tomorrow, so I believe we should take a chance and enjoy life because you never know what tomorrow will bring."

Robert said, "You doing okay? I've never heard you talk like this before. Is everything all right? If you need something, I hope you know you can call me."

I smiled and said, "Thanks. I might take you up on that one day, but not today. But thanks, anyway."

"Okay. Well, keep in touch, and if I hear anything, I'll let you know. Take care," Robert said and hung up.

I went to bed and tossed and turned all night. I got up early and fixed breakfast and checked on George. He was having a bad day. He was sick at his stomach and in pain, so I helped him wash up and get dressed, and I helped him to his chair. He wanted coffee, so I fixed him some, and he drank it, but he wouldn't eat. I told him that if he ate toast, that might help his medicine not to upset his stomach. He ate two slices of toast with his coffee, and then he took his medicine.

I fix Nicky a plate, and he ate and then crawled into George's lap. I tried to get him, but George said he's fine. They watched TV, and they both fell asleep, so I covered them with a blanket and went to clear off the dishes when my phone rang.

It was the detective, and he wanted to see me, but I told him about George's health. He informed me that my mother wasn't sick; she was poison by Clair Williams at the time she was widowed to Samuel Williams, Roberts's dad.

"How could it be that my mother had cancer and she had Clair as her nurse?" I asked the detective, and he said, "Well, your mom and Clair were friends. They both worked at the nursing home, and somehow, Clair started poisoning her, and we checked, and there was no doctor's diagnosis of cancer." He cleared his voice. "We think that Clair had met your dad, and she decided that she wanted him, so she poisoned your mom and somehow covered her tracks by making your mom believe that she had cancer and was dying."

I had tears running down my cheeks. My beautiful and sweet mom, taken away from me by that bitch.

The detective said, "I'm so sorry for your loss on both your mom and dad. If you have any questions, just call me," and then he hung up. I sat at the kitchen table for what seemed like a lifetime, and then she went to check on George and Nicky. They were both sleeping still, so I called Robert. He didn't answer, so I left a message and asked him to call me when he had time. Then I started fixing lunch. By the time I had it ready, Nicky was asking to eat, and I helped George to the table so he could eat too. He seemed to feel better, and after lunch, he asked if Nicky wanted to go to the park. Nicky was so excited, but I suggested we wait until this evening with the heat index so high, but George said we didn't have to stay long, so we went ahead.

I found George a bench seat under the shade, and we watched Nicky play in the sand. He wanted to go down the slide and insisted I go with him. After thirty minutes, I insisted that we go home and cool off. After we got home, I fixed iced tea for George and apple juice for Nicky, and then they retired to the recliner to watch TV. I started cooking dinner. Nicky wanted spaghetti and meatballs, so I had just started cooking when Robert called. "Do you have time to talk?"

I answered, "Yes, I do. The detective called me this morning. Have you heard from him?"

Robert was silent for a moment, and then he said, "I was just at the police station when you called, and they told me everything. I'm so sorry to hear about your mom."

I said, "I was shocked. I never knew that Mom worked with her, and to think that she took my mom from me for no reason other than greed."

Robert said, "I checked into my mom's health, and she had cancer and needed a hysterectomy, but when they exhumed her body, she had poison in her system, and the medical examiner said if they would have done surgery, then she would have been fine."

"Oh, I'm so sorry. Did your mom know Clair?"

"She worked at the hospital on the surgery wing, but they don't know how or why except that she somehow knew my dad had money, and she was after him for his money, and they have inclusive reports on my dad. He had poison in him, but not enough to kill him when he died."

"Oh, how I wish that bitch was still alive so that I could make her pay."

"I know how you feel," Robert said. "I had better let you go."

"Okay, I'll talk to you later. Bye."

"Bye."

I fixed dinner and called out, "George, dinner's ready!" but I got no response. I went in to check on them, and Nicky was crying "Wake up, George, wake up!"

I picked up Nicky and checked George and called 911. Then I called Rachel and asked her to come get Nicky. She and Matt came immediately. Nicky was scared and crying and didn't want to leave my arms, but Matt took him and told him that I had to help George and that he would take him to play on the swing set, and Nicky said okay. I thanked him, and Rachel stayed with me until the ambulance came. She told me to call and that Nicky would be fine.

I rode with George to the hospital. He was so weak, but he smiled at me and held out his hand to me, so I smiled and held his hand all the way to the hospital. The doctor admitted him, and they did blood work and test, and after six hours, the doctor came in and said that George had a heart attack and mild stroke, which was a side effect of his medicine. George told the doctor he was ready to go to be with his wife Sophie and that it was really hard tolerating the pain, and even though I wasn't ready to let him go, I must.

I told him that I'm a big girl and that it was okay, but we would miss him. I said Nicky and I loved him so much, and we will be okay. The doctor said that we could transfer to the hospice floor and that I could stay with him.

George asked to see Nicky first, and I explained the situation to the doctor, who said that it was fine. It was against the rules to let children that young in for visits, but the doctor said he would make an exception. I called Rachel and asked her and Matt to bring Nicky down to see George, and they said they would be here shortly. The nurse gave George something for pain, and when Nicky arrived, he was so excited to see George. I cautioned him not to get too rambunctious, but George said he was fine. Nicky climbed in bed with George, and George told Nicky that he was going home to be with his wife and that he was leaving him in charge of looking after me.

Nicky said, "You can't leave me," and he started crying.

George said, "My wife needs me, so I have to go, but I'll always be thinking of you and your mom, and I'll be watching over you from heaven." George gave Nicky a hug. Nicky said, "I will take care of Mommy, I promise." Then Rachel and Matt took Nicky home with them after Nicky gave hugs to George and me. After they left, George gave me instructions as to what to do and told me that he made vacation plans to go to Gulf Shores next month and that I needed to take Nicky.

I cried, and George said that it would be all right, and I hugged him as I was crying, and he told me to be happy for him; he was going to see Sophie. He dozed off, and I sat with him. My phone vibrated. It was Robert.

I texted him.

Can't talk, bad time. Will call later.

His text back read,

On the way to see you.

My reply was

I'm not home. I'm at the hospital with George.

To which he responded with

Just got off plane. Be there soon.

Robert showed up within an hour, and he said, "George called me after you came home from the park and said that you might need me, so here I am." I stayed with George, and Robert went to the waiting room in case I needed him.

I sat in a chair, holding George's hand, when the alarms went on and the nurses came in and turned them off. Sherry, the head nurse, came to sit with me. She said it wouldn't be long, and she stayed with me until the end. I cried, and she let me stay with him until I was ready to go. As I walked out of his room, Robert was walking toward me, and I fell in his arms, sobbing. He helped me to a seat and held me until I was done crying. Then the nurse brought me George's personal effects, and I cried all the way home.

I walked into the house expecting George there, but he wasn't. I told Robert I had to go get Nicky, and he walked over with me. I introduce Robert to Matt and Rachel, and Nicky was glad to see me and asked where George was. Rachel said, "Remember, Nicky? He went to help his wife in heaven."

Nicky said, "I forgot. I'm going to miss George. Do you think he'll remember me?"

Matt said, "Of course, he will, and he'll be watching over you and your mommy from heaven."

That was the first time that I realized that I'm fulfilling a role as a mom. They gave us hugs, and we took Nicky home, and I got him ready for bed. Nicky got up and came into the living room, and he hugged me and said, "I'll take care of you, Mommy, and Robert will help me. George told me so."

I smiled and said, "Yes. George always knew what was happening. Give me a kiss and go to bed."

He hugged and kissed me, and then he gave Robert a hug and off to bed he went. I told Robert that he could sleep in my room. I wanted to sleep on the couch like I did several times when George was having a bad day or night, but Robert said he would sleep on the couch. I needed to get some sleep, so I got him a blanket and a pillow, and he gave me a kiss and said good night.

I didn't sleep well at all. I tossed and turned all night, and then when I finally fell asleep, I dreamed that George was falling, and I was trying to catch his hand but couldn't reach him. I must have cried out in my sleep because I realized that I was crying, and Robert was holding me and comforting me. I held on to him as if I was falling, and after I quit crying, he tilted my face up and kissed me so gently, and I kissed him back and the passion grew and before I knew what I was doing, we were in bed making love. He was so gentle and loving, and I just needed him so much. Afterward, I fell asleep. He held me, but when I woke up, I was in bed by myself. I got a quick shower and went downstairs.

As much as the pain that I was in with losing George, I felt like maybe, finally, I found the love of my life, but I won't get ahead of myself. I have some difficult days ahead of me. Robert was cooking bacon and eggs with Nicky's help.

Robert said, "Just in time. I have everything done with the help of Nicky."

I smiled and asked Nicky, "What help did you do?" He said, "I told him my favorite was bacon and eggs, so he cooked them," and then he giggled, so I hugged him. We ate breakfast, and I helped clean up the kitchen. Then I called the priest and the funeral home and made an appointment to go in and set everything up. Robert was supportive and caring and helped with Nicky. When it was time to go to the funeral home, Rachel came over to get Nicky so that Robert could go with me. I was so glad I was almost in tears all morning. To keep pretending that everything was fine was hard to keep up. Mr. Linsey at the funeral home was an older gentleman, and he said he knew George for over sixty years. They were neighbors growing up, and Sophie was his girlfriend first in the second grade, but once she fell for George, there was no going back. They were in love from second grade, all the way through marriage, through having a son and losing him, and even through her passing, and George loved her until the end. When filling out the paperwork, he said that it was George and Sophie's anniversary on May 12. I wondered if maybe George remembered. George had made most of the arrangements already, so all I had to do was pick out flowers and the coffin. I asked Mr. Linsey if they had one similar to Sophie's, and he said yes, and it was called eternal love. Where Sophie's was light pink with flowers etched in, George's was light blue with the words "Love is eternal." There was a space where you could put names, so I picked that and asked to put George and Sophie's names with their marriage date. I also asked if they could put their picture on their headstone with a picture of their son, and Mr. Linsey said yes and that he would take care of it. I ordered red roses, and I brought a picture of George with me and Nicky and asked if they could use that picture with us in it, and he said he could. After we got everything done, I asked what I owed, but he said that George left payment already and that there was probably some money coming back to me. On the way home, we stopped and had lunch at the deli.

Robert asked me, "Are you okay?"

I said, "No. I lost my best friend, and I don't know how to go on by myself."

Robert frowned and said, "He was just a kind old man Melissa. He wasn't your family, and I'm not sure why you're taking it so hard."

I looked up and said, "He was my family and has been for over six years. How can you be so uncaring? Haven't you ever had someone who meant the world to you? I feel sorry for you Robert, that you never knew George. He was the kindest man I ever met, and the day I met him, he and Sophie, his wife, was in a terrible car accident, and he lost his wife that day, and I was lucky enough to be there to help him when he needed someone."

Robert looked put out and said, "If you would have given your father that much love and caring, maybe you too would have been close instead of running away from your real family."

"I've had enough of you. I'm calling a cab and going home. I suggest you come get your things and be on your way. I don't need a lecture on family. I didn't run away; I was run off and my dad did nothing to stop it."

Robert said, "I didn't mean to upset you, but the irony of the situation is awkward, and I'm not sure how to deal with it."

"I'm going home," I said, and I got up and walked out. Robert threw money on the table and ran after me. "Melissa, I'll take you home, and I'll stay if you want me to."

I turned and looked at him and said, "You can drop me off, and you need to get your things and go back where you belong because it's not with me."

Robert tried talking to me on the way back to the house, but I sat there and ignored him. How could I think that I was falling in love with him? He was a jerk, and I don't remember him saying that he loved me while we made love.

We got back to the house, and Robert asked, "Can we talk? You're just emotional. I understand you lost a friend and are upset, but after last night, I think you owe me some consideration."

I turned and said, "I think you need to go," and I walked upstairs and went to my bedroom, shut the door, lay down, and cried. I was glad that I called Rachel to check on Nicky, and she said her grandkids were over, so if it was okay, she would keep him all day, and maybe I could get some rest. I went downstairs later in the afternoon, and Robert was gone. There was a note, and it read:

Melissa:
If you need me call, if I don't hear from you, I won't bother you again.
Sign Robert

I fixed me a cup of tea and took Tylenol and went back to bed and cried myself to sleep. I woke up, and it was after six, so I called Rachel. She told me the kids were watching a movie and eating pizza, and they wanted Nicky to stay the night unless I wanted him home, but I told her that it was fine and that I appreciate everything they were doing. I ate grilled cheese and then went to bed.

I got up early the next morning; I had so much to do. George's service was starting tonight at four, and I had to go get Nicky an outfit and me a dress. I had several calls today about the arrangements. I had posted it in the newspaper, and several of his colleagues had called, sent flowers, and cards. I called Rachel around nine, and she was feeding the kids breakfast and said Matt would bring Nicky over in about thirty minutes. I showered, changed into a light blue suit, and Shelly called and said she was coming by in a few minutes. She offered to come with me and help with Nicky. She had talked to Sally and that she was heartbroken and wish she could be here for me and Nicky, and she said she would call me late tonight to check on me. Matt brought Nicky, and Shelly gave him a quick bath and dressed him for me while I answered the phone and the door.

The funeral director called and said that there were so many flowers and gifts of symphony that they had to move to the largest room. We finally got to go shopping, and I found a little navy suit for Nicky, and I bought a navy dress with a jacket for me. I remembered when I took George shopping for his arrangements. He picked a navy suit with a navy tie and white shirt, and he joked about me buying a matching outfit. I missed George so much; he was the only family I had, but now, all I have is Nicky.

The bank called and needed to see me as soon as possible, so I had Shelly drop me off and take Nicky to McDonald's for lunch. I planned that when I was done, I would walk over. The bank got my message about George, and they wanted to give their condolences and let me know that George had everything set up for me and Nicky and that if I needed anything, I could just call them. The bank manager told me that George left me his safety deposit box and that I was to get it as soon as possible, so I sat in a small room, and the bank manager Russell brought it to me and told me to take my time. I sat in the chair as if in a dream. How could

George be gone? I opened the box, and there was a note from George. He wanted me to have Sophie jewelry. and he had something special made just for me: it was a sapphire necklace, an earring, a bracelet, and a ring. He had it specially commissioned for me as a genuine thank you for always being there, and he wanted me to know how much he loved me and thought of me as his daughter. I sat there looking at this beautiful gesture, and I remembered George told me once that I had midnight blue eyes, just like sapphires, and that he had never seen anyone with that color blue before. I gathered my wits about me, wiped my eyes, and blew my nose, and I thanked Russell and went to meet Shelly and Nicky. Shelly was in shock and amazed over the jewelry. We returned home, and there were flowers delivered to the house. They were red roses with white carnations dipped in red and sprayed with glitter. I looked to see who sent them here, but instead of the funeral home, they were from Robert. The card read, "If you get lonely and need me, just call I'll be around. Robert."

Shelly said, "Those are gorgeous. He must be crazy over you."

I said, "No, he just wants to outdo George, and he can go to hell as far as I'm concerned"

"But George is gone, and George thought of you as a daughter. Is he serious? I can't imagine anybody being jealous of George." Shelly said.

"Robert is screwed up. He doesn't think like a rational man," I said, and then I looked at my watch. "I had better start getting ready." Then I looked at Shelly. "Are you coming tonight?"

Shelly nodded and said, "I'll be there. I can help with Nicky, and that will make it easier on you." Then she gave me a hug and told me to "hang in there" before leaving.

I changed into a black suit and remembered how George always told me I looked like one of the Men in Black, which was one of his favorite movies. I dressed Nicky in a black pair of jeans with a black shirt, and then tomorrow, we will dress up George for the service.

The viewing started at four, and Nicky and I got there around three so that we could spend some quiet time. I also wanted to prepare Nicky if he had any questions. We walked in the funeral home, and Nicky took my hand and said, "If George is in heaven helping his wife, why we are here to see him?"

The funeral director said, "May I explain to him?" I looked at him and smiled and said thanks. He took Nicky to sit on a small couch, and he explained that "Once we get to heaven, our body doesn't, so that's how everybody gets to say their goodbyes. You don't need to be scared because George is in heaven watching over you and Missy."

Nicky said he wasn't scared anymore and that he was ready to see George, so I took him in. He held my hand tightly, but he was very brave. I sat looking at George, and Nicky said, "Our clothes match, Mommy. Do you think George sees us?"

I said, "I'm sure he does, and he will always be watching over us." Nicky and I walked around looking at all the flowers, plants, and gifts. There was so many that I lost count, and they brought about another ten or so while we waited until four. Then people started showing up, and it got to be a bit much, but I stood my ground and greeted everyone and heard all kinds of stories. Shelly showed up and took Nicky with her so that she could feed him. I met so many people that I lost count and forgot names. Rachel and Matt showed up and stayed until late and took Nicky home with them, and Rachel said that she would call me in the morning around nine. The viewing started at eleven in the morning, and the service started at two, so when everybody was gone, I sat with George and talked with him.

"George, I love you and miss you so much. I wish you were my father. You loved me and treated me like your daughter since the first day I met you. I wish we had more time together, but I have so many memories and I'll treasure them forever." Then I went home all alone and changed into my pajamas and cried myself to sleep.

I woke up early, showered, and changed into my navy dress and laid out Nicky's navy outfit. I fixed my coffee, and there was a knock at the door. As I got close to the door, I could see there were several people standing on the porch. As I opened the door, there was Ms. Margaret, Charles, Trina, and Mrs. Tinsley. I ran into Margaret's arms and almost cried. I said in a very emotional voice, "What are you all doing here?"

Mrs. Tinsley said, "Mr. Robert called and said that you needed someone, so we decided that maybe you needed all of us."

I smiled and hugged each of them and said, "Yes, I do, and I'm so glad to see you all. Please come in." I took them into the living room, and then Matt called and said he was bringing Nicky over so everyone could get to see him and how much he'd grown. Trina asked if she could bathe him and help him get ready, and Nicky said, "I bathe myself, but you can help me if you want." While they were gone, I caught up with the others. It was almost nine, and I said that I needed to get to the funeral home. They said that they would go with us in case I needed anything, and it felt really good to have them here with me. When we got to the funeral home, there had been more gifts and flowers delivered, and the director asked if I could choose the music, so I gave him the list of songs that I picked. The priest wanted to talk to me, so I excused myself and went to talk to him. He wanted to go over the service and make sure he didn't leave anything out. He told me that George left a message to be read in the service, and I told him that it was fine. The letter was about George, and with my eyes tearing up, the priest gave me some tissues. I thanked him, then I started greeting people.

There were so many people who came to the wake, but I lost count when it was time for the service. The funeral director opened up another room that was connected to this one, but it had movable walls so that it could accommodate as many guests as possible. Rachel and Matt helped with Nicky, and right before the service started, Nicky ran over to me and asked, "Can I talk to George?"

I looked surprised, and the priest said, "Do you mind if I take him up to talk with George?"

"No, that would be fine," I said. Nicky grabbed my hand, and the three of us went up to the coffin. Nicky said, "George, I miss and love you. I promise to take care of Mommy and say my prayers every night. Give your Sophie a hug and a kiss from us, and if you get time, can you check on us sometimes? Goodbye, George. I will miss you, and I will keep Mommy safe."

I had tears running down my cheeks. Nicky smiled, and I picked him up, hugged him, and kissed his cheek. I said, "I will miss George also, but we have each other, and we can do this, and I'm so proud of you."

We took our seats as the music started. The service ran rather long with the songs and the eulogy, and the priest read a message from George. It read:

After the service, it took a while for everyone to clear out before going to the cemetery. Nicky and I rode in the white family car with the priest, and there were over thirty cars that followed. The graveside service was short, and I didn't remember George being in the military, but they did the flag and the firing of the guns, and that scared Nicky, so he climbed into my lap. The funeral director handed red roses out to Nicky and I, and then he handed them out to other guests. We rode back to the funeral home where my car was, and the director wanted to know where to deliver the flowers and gifts, so I gave him the address. I took Nicky to St. Mary's Catholic Church for the reception afterwards. Shelly fixed Nicky's food, and Ms. Margaret fixed me a plate. I picked at the food; it was good, but I wasn't hungry. Nicky had several people helping him—Trina, Rachel, Matt, and Shelly—so I didn't have to worry about him. My voice was hoarse by the time we had to leave. I cried so much and talked with so many of George's friends and colleagues. I was glad when I could finally get Nicky and go home. Margaret offered to come home with me, but I told her I needed some time alone, and she understood. I told her to come tomorrow, and she said that they would.

I took Nicky home, and he was so tired. I gave him a quick bath help him into his pajamas, and I fixed him a bowl of cereal. After eating, he said, "Good night. I love you, Mommy," to which I replied, "I love you too, baby." He went to his room and was fast asleep.

I went downstairs and fixed myself a cup of tea and sat on the couch, just too tired to do anything else. The last few days took their tow on me, and I didn't know what to do next. I decided to go to bed, so I put my cup in the sink, but my phone rang. It was Robert. "Hello?"

Robert said, "I called to check on you. How are you holding up?"

"I'm fine. I just got Nicky down, and I'm fixing to go to bed. Thank you for sending Margaret and the gang here for me," I said.

"I thought you might need someone to talk to and to help you through this."

"That was kind of you, considering how I feel, so thank you again."

"I only want you to be happy, and I know you're miserable now, but one day you'll be happy again. I'll let you get to bed. Call me if you need anything," said Robert, and he hung up.

I went to bed, but my phone rang again. This time, it was Sally calling to check on me and Nicky. We talked for a while, and after I got off the phone, I went to sleep.

In the morning, I got up and showered, and I dressed into jeans and a tank top. I fried bacon and eggs with hot cakes, and then I went to check on Nicky. He was lying in bed, crying. I hurried over to him, and he crawled into my lap. "What's the matter, sweetie? Why the tears?" I asked, and Nicky said, "I miss George. He was my only friend, and now he's gone."

I rubbed his back and said, "You have plenty of friends. You have Rachel, Matt, their grandson Cody and Jeff. Plus, you have Shelly and me."

Nicky said, "George was my best friend."

"I know how you feel. George was my best friend also, but he would want us to make other friends. And you know, next year, you'll got to preschool, and you'll make all kinds of friends there."

"Are you sure?"

I smiled and hugged him, and I said, "I'm very sure. Now let's go downstairs and have breakfast. I made bacon."

We ate breakfast, and then the funeral home called, and they said they were bringing over the things from the funeral. Margaret, Charles, Trina, and Mrs. Tinsley came over at ten, and just as we sat down to have coffee, the vans arrived to unload all the flowers and gifts that people sent for George. I didn't realize that there would be so much; it took three vans' load and a car. They carried in all the gifts, and they put several trees and huge plants on the porch. They brought in wind chimes, several throws, angels, figurines, silk, flowers, pictures, and so much more. I was a little overwhelmed by everything. I asked the director what I was supposed to do with everything, and he told me to sort out what I want to keep and then sell or donate everything else. I asked Trina to take Nicky to the park to play, while Margaret, Charles, and Mrs. Tinsley helped me figure out these things.

I called Shelly to see if she could come and help, so she, Mrs. Tinsley, and Margaret helped me sort, and Charles carried them as we separated what I wanted to keep. Trina brought Nicky home, and Rachel called to see if Nicky wanted to go to McDonald's with Matt and the boys.

Rachel came over to help us out. By late afternoon, we had a few things that I thought Nicky would like to keep to remember George by, and I picked out what I wanted and offered Shelly and the others if they wanted anything. Shelly took an angel with the Lord's prayer on it, and Rachel took a concrete statue of an angel watching over the children, but no one else wanted anything. I decided to donate the rest to the senior home where one of George's friend resides. We went several times visiting, and because of his health, he couldn't come to the funeral. I called the senior home and asked if they could have someone pick the things up, and they said they would be out early next morning to pick them up, and they thanked me. I ordered pizza for a late lunch, and everyone was starving. Mrs. Tinsley, Trina, Margaret, and Charles said their goodbyes, and said they were leaving early in the morning. After Shelly left, Rachel and I sat talking until Matt came home with the boys. Nicky wanted to stay the night with the boys, and Rachel and Matt said that he could, so I packed him a small bag, and he gave me hugs and kisses, and then I was all by myself. I showered and put on a blue sundress, and I went out to get something to eat. I went to Shackles Steak House and ordered a salad bar and ribs. I ate a salad, some part of baked potato, and half of the ribs. I wasn't paying attention to anything in the steak house until I heard someone call my name. I looked up and saw Joe heading my way. I used to ride with him and his wife Charlee sometimes until his wife got sick and passed away with cancer. I got up and gave him a hug and asked, "What are you doing here? I thought you were living in Florida."

Joe laughed and said, "I missed home, so I came back. I was there about six months and missed going to see Sheila and putting flowers out for her."

"I went by and cleaned her stone and put flowers out a few times until George got sick," I said.

"I heard about him. I'm so sorry. George was a good man. He helped a lot of people, and when Charlee passed away, George help me with the cost of her funeral."

I smiled. "He was very generous man. He liked helping everybody. I tried to help take care of him when he and Sophie had their wreck. He was lost without her, but the more I helped him, the more he helped me too. He treated me like a daughter. I miss him so much."

Joe reached over and squeezed my hand and said, "He told me several times that if it wasn't for you, he wouldn't be here today. He loved you very much. He told me once that he and Sophie wanted a girl so much, but after she had James, she couldn't have any more children, but they were grateful to have James. And when they lost him, it nearly destroyed them, but we all were there for them. I had just gotten my bike, and I had ridden with James on several trips, and the day he got killed, he was sitting still, waiting for the light to change, when a drunk driver turned in front of a pickup and tried to avoid hitting it, and instead, it hit James."

"I didn't know. George never talked about James very much. I know they kept his room exactly the way he left it. I couldn't imagine losing Nicky," I said.

Joe smiled. "How's Nicky doing? I bet he's really growing up."

I asked Joe to join me, and we talked. Joe ordered dinner, and when his food came, I finished eating with him, and we talked all the way through dinner. I insisted that we get dessert, so we ordered a brownie surprise for two. I had a nice time, and I was really glad that I ran into Joe. Joe walked me out to my car, and he was parked behind me. He showed me his new bike and asked if I had been riding lately, but I told him my bike was still in Pennsylvania, so he offered to give me a ride. I told him that I wasn't ready to show my ass off to the world yet, and he laughed; but I told him to come by one day, and I would go with him. I gave him a hug and a kiss and said good night, and I went home feeling better than before I went out.

After I got home, I showered and put on my night gown and fixed me a cup of tea. I sat to watch the news, and then there was a banging on my door, so I hurried in case it was Matt and had to tell me about Nicky, but instead, it was Robert, standing there and looking pissed off.

"Oh, it's you. What do you want, Robert?" I said. Robert replied, "Who did you expect? That brut you were with earlier?"

"Excuse me. It's none of your business who I'm with, and how did you know I was out with someone?" I demanded.

"I saw you let that guy paw you, and you even responded to him. Poor George, he hasn't been gone a week, and you're out trolling for men already," Robert said nastily. Without thinking, I slapped him across the face.

"How dare you? You have no right to talk to me like that! That brut you talk about is a good friend of mine, and I don't owe you an explanation, so you need to leave, and don't bother coming back." I went to shut the door, but Robert pushed it open and grabbed and kissed me hard and punishing, and I tried to fight but I realized that I wanted him to kiss me and how I long for it. The kiss turned into passion I responded with, and before I knew it, we were throwing off our clothes. Robert lay me on the couch, and we made hot, passionate love, or so I thought.

Our passion and pain converged into something I had never experienced before, and it went on over and over again until we were both exhausted. I fell asleep with Robert on the couch, and when I woke up, he was gone. No note, nothing. Maybe he'll call me in the morning, I thought. I went to bed and dreamed about Robert, and I realized that somehow, I had fallen in love with him.

When I woke up, I showered and dressed in jeans and T-shirt, and I went downstairs for coffee. There was a message on the answering service, and thinking it was from Robert, I got excited. It wasn't what I expected, but it was indeed from Robert:

I am ashamed of what happened. I never realized you were such a whore and would act the way you do with just anybody. You have no self-respect for yourself or anybody else. I'm turning over the house and everything with it to you. I hope to never see you again. Robert

I stood there with tears running down my face. How he could be so cruel? Well, I'm glad that I know where I stand with him. I went upstairs and cried myself to sleep. I woke up after ten and called Rachel to see how Nicky was doing, and she said they were eating breakfast, and then Matt would be taking them to the park, and afterward, he would bring him home. Rachel asked if I was all right because I sounded like I had been crying. I told her that it was a long story but that I'll be all right.

I spent the day cleaning and going through George's bedroom. I threw away his junk mail and medications. I went through his mail and sent in some bills and notified all his business contacts that he had passed, and then I fixed meat loaf for dinner and put it in the oven and made mashed potatoes and green beans. Matt brought Nicky home around four, and he said that Nicky went with him to take the boys home. I invited him and Rachel over for dinner, and he said he'd check with Rachel, and he would have her call me. Nicky talked nonstop about all the fun he had with the boys, and then he asked if he could have a brother. I told him not right now, but maybe later on, when I find us someone to complete our family. I told him that it might not be a brother and it could be a sister, and he said "Yuck! Then I don't want one!" and I laughed with that.

I started his laundry and finished dinner when Rachel and Matt came over. Rachel helped me set the table, while Matt watched cartoons with Nicky. Rachel asked if I was okay, and I told her that I had been insulted and got my feelings hurt, but now I got over it. Then I told her what Nicky asked of me, and we both laughed.

Rachel said, "It's always nice to be young and think you can go to the grocery and pick up a brother or sister."

I laughed. "Yeah, like I could handle another child, I'm still learning with Nicky, and now I'm all alone."

"You're not alone. You have us, and if you need anything, all you have to do is ask." Rachel said, and I thanked her and gave her a hug.

Dinner was good, and we had a nice time. After Rachel and Matt left, I watched cartoons with Nicky. I gave him a bath and helped him with his pajamas, and then he kissed me good night and went to bed. I stayed up and did the dishes and cleaned the kitchen, and then I got out the thank you cards and visitation book and started sorting out the thank you notes. I worked on them until two in the morning, and I was only one-fourth of the way done.

I slept in and got up after nine, and I checked on Nicky, and he was playing in his room. He said I was sleeping so he didn't want to wake me up. I fixed breakfast and after we ate, I took Nicky to grocery shopping. Nicky liked shopping. We always went to Costco, and he liked to try the different foods their demoing. Nicky tried chicken, steak, shrimp, and pizza. After we checked out, we got soft drinks and ice-cream before we left the store. After we got home and unloaded the car, there was a message on the answering service, so I waited until Nicky went to play before I listened to it in case it was another nasty message from Robert; but it was Stanley Miller, George's friend and attorney, who said he wanted to come by today and go over George's will. I called him, and he came over after lunch.

"Hi, Stanley. Good to see you." I said.

"Hello Missy, how are you doing? I meant to check on you sooner, but work has been keeping me busy." Stanley said, and I smiled. "Thank you, but we're doing okay. We miss George, and I know he's in a better place, but the house is so quiet, and we get lonely."

"I know what you mean. When my Betty passed away, I couldn't stand being at home by myself, but I did finally get used to her not being there, and I know you and Nicky will do okay. It just takes time adjusting."

"Thank you. George has been there for me for over six years. He was all the family I had," I said.

Stanley asked, "Is little Nicky doing okay?"

I smiled. "Yes, for the most part. He came down last night to tell me and George good night, and he apologized, but I told him that was okay. I miss George also."

"I'm sure. But I had better get to the job at hand," Stanley said. "I brought a copy of the will so that I could go over it with you. George left everything to you. He did call after he found out about the cancer and added Nicky. You get the house and all of its contents, the car, truck, jeep, and the lake house and the Florida house with the contents, the car and SUV down there, plus, you get a time share that's paid off, and I have all the deeds, and they have been put into your name. George also left you all his money, and he set aside $500,000 to Nicky, at which you have discretionary over when he gets it."

"I had no idea he had all that. I thought he had a house and car. What am I to do with all this, Stanley? I don't need the money, the property, or anything else. I don't know what I'm doing from day-to-day, let alone be able to know how to take care of any of this," I said, a little overwhelmed.

Stanley said, "Not to worry. George said if you want to sell everything, he was okay with that. He only wanted to help you be self-sufficient and not have to worry about anything but raising Nicky. He thought of you as a daughter, and he said there are very few that would take the time to set with a stranger and help him grieve for his wife and constantly check on him and help him get through such a bad time. And you kept taking care of him like how a daughter would. He loved you and Nicky very much, so I will leave all these things with you, and you take your time and let me know if you want to sell anything, or if you just want to talk or need any guidance, I'll be here for you. I don't know if I told you, but when my Betty passed away, George sat with me, and he helped me get through such a difficult time. He was a great man, and he had a great daughter," Stanley said. "Goodbye. Call if you need me. Oh, by the way, George had made arrangements for a two-week vacation at Gulf Shores. Everything's paid for and set up. I think he knew his time was close because he made plans for you and Nicky only. There's a big white envelope with all the directions, plans, and everything you two need. Call me if you need anything."

I gave him a hug and said, "Thank you," and then he left. I sat at the kitchen table and looked through the papers and decided that it was just a nice day to take Nicky to the park. It was rather hot, but Nicky had a good time until some older kids showed up and was yelling at the little ones and started pushing the smaller kids. I got up and walked over and told them they didn't have to be so mean, and one boy, about fifteen or so, pushed me and called me all kinds of names, so I called 911. This kid told Nicky that he would come in his window and split his throat one night, and then they ran off. I took pictures of them and when the police arrived, I told them what they were doing and what they said, and I showed him the pictures of the boys. The officer wasn't surprised; he had problems with the family before, but he said he would go by again, and the officer told Nicky not to worry and that he won't let them hurt him. Nicky gave the officer a hug.

I took Nicky out to dinner, and we went to Chuck E. Cheese's. After he ate, he played and had a good time. We had just got home a little after seven, and I told Nicky to go watch TV. Rachel called and asked if Nicky could come over and stay the night since her boys just got there, and they were staying for a few days, so I asked Nicky if he wanted to go there and stay the night. He said yes, and he went upstairs and got his bag, put his pajamas in it with his favorite bear, and came back down. I went to the laundry room and was getting him some clothes to put in his bag when Matt came over to get him. He gave me a kiss and asked if I will be okay if he goes to Matt's house, and I gave him hugs and kissed him and told him I'd be fine.

I sat down and started on the thank you cards again, and I worked on them until it was done. It was going on six in the morning, and I counted them and there were over three hundred of them. I went and lay down and fell asleep. My phone rang at nine that morning, and it was Joe, and he wanted to know if I wanted to go riding. He was coming at two to get me, so I took a nap and got up at eleven. I showered, dressed in jeans and my Harley tank top and cowboy boots. I braided my hair and was on the porch waiting for Joe when he pulled up. I had called and checked on Nicky, and Rachel said they were camping out in the back yard tonight and that they were all so excited. I told her I was going out riding with Joe and told her to leave me a message if they needed me. We rode to Hanover and down to Sidney Lake for about a two-hour ride. We ate in a fish house, rode through Beth Haven, and then went home. We got home after nine, so I asked Joe to come in for coffee and cake, so we talked and watched a scary movie. Joe left after one, and then I went to bed.

I slept greatly that night. I woke up and showered and dressed into a purple romper, and then I went outside and mowed my yard. When George was here, he hired someone to mow his yard, but I would rather mow myself. I fixed me a glass of lemonade before I got the weed eater and started on the yard. I was just starting the front when Matt came running over, and I could tell there was something wrong. "Matt, what's the matter?" "Nicky got stung by bees in the yard," Matt said. "I think you need to take him to ER."

I dropped the weed eater and ran over to check on Nicky. He was stung on the hand and wrist and was crying in pain. Rachel had an ice pack, treating him gently, and she went with me to St. Joseph Hospital. They took him in immediately, and the doctors came in and gave Nicky a shot to counteract the sting and said it would make him sleepy. They kept him overnight for observation and to make sure he had no complications to the bee sting or the medicine. I thanked Rachel for bringing us and sent her home. She said that Matt would come to get us in the morning when we were ready. Nicky slept for the rest of the day and most of the night. Joe called, and I told him about Nicky getting stung, and he came by to visit and brought me dinner. After he left, I dozed off in the chair and remembered all the times I was here with George and how I missed him. They let us leave after lunch the next day, and Joe came by and got us. We got Nicky settled in, and his hand was sore, but he seemed okay while watching cartoons. I fixed dinner, and Joe went out and finished my yard while I cooked. I called Rachel and asked if they would like to come for dinner. I fixed hamburgers and French fries for the boys, and I chilled wine for me and Rachel and put beer in the refrigerator for the guys. The kids ate and watched cartoons, and Matt told me about the hornets' nest in the yard by the kids' sandbox, so he had the exterminator come. He apologized, but I told him it wasn't his fault.

We played cards after dinner. I told Rachel about the two-week vacation that George sat up for us, and she said they would keep a watch over the house while we were gone. Rachel and Matt carried the boys home, and Joe carried the little girl for them. The kids had fallen asleep along with Nicky watching TV. When Joe came back, he carried Nicky upstairs and put him in his bed. We watched the news, and as Joe left to go home, he kissed me good night. I took a quick shower and dressed for bed, and as I lay in bed, I thought about the kiss. It was nice, but it wasn't like Robert's kiss. Robert's kiss had passion and an urgency to consume every thought and feeling—a need to ecstasy. I fell asleep and dreamed of Robert and his passion and lovemaking and how he despised me. How could I fall for someone I hardly knew?

I woke with a headache, and I felt nauseous. I checked on Nicky, and he was upstairs playing in his room. I dressed and went downstairs to make breakfast.

Nicky and I got into a routine, and we were going on vacation in ten days. It will be good to get away and relax. We shopped for bathing suits, shorts, and tank tops. I packed up the car, and after telling everyone goodbye, we went to Gulf Shores.

The condo was amazing. George had planned shows, dinner, and the petting zoo, and we laid around the beach and pools. We really had a wonderful time, but we missed George terribly. The whole time away, I wasn't sick at all, but as soon as we came back, my stomach got upset. I was having trouble sleeping and I was moody.

Rachel and Matt were glad we were back, and life went on. We were home almost a week before I thought about calling Joe to come for dinner.

As the weeks went by, Joe became a regular visitor, and Nicky and Joe became great friends. Everything was good, except that I was feeling under the weather. I had headaches and feeling sick at my stomach; I lost appetite and lost weight. Joe insisted I go see a doctor to make sure it wasn't something serious, so I went to see my family doctor. They did blood work and went over my history and family history, and Dr. Neal gave me a full examination.

After I got dressed, the nurse sent me to Dr. Neal's office to talk. As I sat down, something told me that there was a problem. I asked, "Is everything good, Doctor? Did you find any problems?"

"No, not really. Except that you've lost twelve pounds in two months, but everything checks out fine. Your blood work should be in here in a few minutes. It could be stress from your friend passing, and grief can cause a lot of health concerns, so maybe you need a vacation. Take some time away from everyday life and go to Florida and lay on the beach and soak up some sun. You look pale, so it could only help," Dr. Neal said.

"I just got back from Gulf Shores," I said.

"Maybe you need a longer time. Were you sick on vacation?" Dr. Neal asked

"No, not much. Some nausea, but most the time, I felt good."

Dr. Neal looked over the papers that the nurse brought in, and then he looked up and said, "Did you know you're pregnant?"

I was in total shock. I looked at him and said, "What? I can't be! There's just no way."

"According to the blood work, you are," Dr. Neal said. "I need for you to set up a first prenatal appointment for next week."

The doctor gave me a prescription for prenatal vitamins, and I set up an appointment for next Friday and for four weeks later. I got in the car and drove to the cemetery where George was laid to rest. I had asked a concrete bench to be placed there at the foot so that when Nicky and I came with flowers each week, we could sit and tell him about our week. "Oh George, what am I going to do? A baby! Can you see me raising two children? I just don't know what to do. I can't tell Robert. He doesn't want anything to do with me. I just don't know what to do. I miss you so much. You were my calm place. You always help me figure out what to do, and I don't know if I can do this by myself," I said, as I pulled up grass and weeds around George's and Sophia's headstones.

I drove home slowly. Joe was watching Nicky, and they had plans on going out to dinner at Buckaroo's, one of Nicky's favorite places. When I arrived home, there was a note from Joey. He had taken Nicky to the park and would be home around four, so I showered and put on light blue cotton jeans and a white T-shirt. I put a little makeup on and put on the necklace that George had gotten me, and I sprayed my favorite perfume. Just then, I saw a piece of paper sticking out of the back of the dresser, so I pulled it, and it was a handwritten note from George. He had written it when we first started going to the doctor and when Nicky and I had first moved in with him. He was glad of the company and I wouldn't have changed anything in the world; I will always treasure my time with George. I read his letter, and my eyes got misty. It read:

Dear Missy,

I'm so overwhelmed with joy that my journey home to Sophie is happening. I just worry about you being all alone. I know you'll have little Nicky, but you need a man in your life. You need a companion, a friend, a lover, someone to grow old with. I wish you all the best, and when the time comes and I'm gone, be happy for me and look forward to your life and build you the life you want and need. You're a wonderful mother, and you have such a big heart filled with love, so take a chance on love. I love you so much. You're the daughter I never had, and I'll always watch over you.

Love, George

I sat down on the side of my bed and cried. I missed George so much, and he's right. I have my guardian angel watching over me, so I had better get my act together. I was downstairs when Joe and Nicky came home, and Nicky gave me a big hug and a kiss. "Hello, Mommy. I missed you."

I smiled. "I missed you too. Why don't you go up and get ready, and we'll go to Buckaroo's?" He went running up the stairs, and Joe sat down at the table and smiled. "That boy's crazy over you. You're so lucky. Hey, what did the doctor say?" Joe asked.

I smiled and said, "Everything's fine. I'm pregnant."

Joe's eyes got big. "Wow! I didn't see that coming!" He smiled. "Are you happy about the baby?"

"I don't know. I'm still in shock," I said. I hadn't told Joe what had happened between me and Robert. I just told him we had a one-night stand and that he was a jerk.

"Are you going to tell that jerk?" Joe asked.

"I don't know, but I have decided that I'm having this baby," I said. "Are you okay with it?"

Joe smiled. "Yes, I'm okay with it. You know how I feel about you, but I didn't want to rush you. We'll do this your way. No pressure, okay?"

I reached over and held his hand and smiled, "I'm glad I told you I wasn't sure what I was going to do, but I'm going to take it one day at a time."

They went out to eat. Nicky ate quickly, so he could play video games. He and Joe played together, and we watched cartoons while we ate, and then they played more games. While waiting for them, there was a tap on my shoulder. It was Shelly, and she gave me a hug and sat down so we could catch up. She told me about meeting a guy that was really sweet and how she really liked him, but there was a problem. I smiled and asked, "What kind of a problem?"

Shelly said, "You know him. It's Robert."

I must have looked shocked because Shelly said, "Don't be mad, please. If you want I'll stop seeing him. Your friendship means a lot to me, and you have helped me so many times. I wasn't sure if I should tell you, but then I saw you sitting here, so I took it as a sign to tell you."

I cleared her throat and said, "You can see whoever you want. I only want you to be happy, and if Robert makes you happy, then that's great." We talked for a few more minutes, and then I said, "I needed to get the boys and get home. It's getting late. It was good to see you. Come by sometime and visit." I gave Shelly a hug and went looking for Joe and Nicky.

Nicky didn't want to leave, but I told him it was time to go, and he said okay. Nicky fell asleep on the way home, and Joe carried him in and put him to bed. Joe asked, "Are you okay? You look like you're upset. Did I do something wrong?"

I smiled and said, "No, you didn't do anything. I'm just tired."

Joe said, "Okay. If you need anything, call me. I'll check in on you tomorrow." He kissed me on the cheeks and left. I was glad that tomorrow was Sunday so that maybe I could sleep in. I locked up and went to bed after checking on Nicky, and I was so glad that I didn't mention being pregnant to Shelly.

When I woke up, I had a headache and felt nauseous. I checked on Nicky, but he was up and was playing with his train, so I went downstairs and made coffee. I decided that maybe we would do cereal today instead of bacon and eggs, so I fixed myself come cereal and milk and ate breakfast. I was rinsing my bowl when Nicky came in. "I don't smell bacon," he said, looking so disappointed.

I said, "We're doing cereal and milk today. Mommy's not feeling good. Is that okay?"

Nicky gave Missy a hug and smiled and said, "Yes, that fine. I'll have Cocoa Krispies, please." Afterward, he went over to play with the boys over at Rachel's, so I cleaned up the house and was starting laundry when I heard a knock. I yelled, "Come in," thinking it was Joe. I turned around, and instead of Joe, it was Robert standing there. "I didn't realize it was you. What do you want Robert?" I said uncaringly.

"I thought we needed to talk. Shelly said she saw you and told you that we are seeing each other," he said.

"I don't care who you see. I just don't want you to hurt Shelly. She may think you're her knight in shining armor, but we both know you can be mean and hateful, and she doesn't deserve that from you or anyone else," I said.

"It's not serious. We're just dating," Robert said defensively.

"You may not be serious, but Shelly thinks you are," I said. "If you're just leading her on with no intention of building a life with her, then you ought to be ashamed."

Robert said hatefully, "After you, why would I get serious with anybody?"

"I don't know how I wronged you, but you can get out now. I don't want you here, and I don't need this crap right now, so just get out." I said, and then I turned and ran to the bathroom so I could throw up.

When I returned to the kitchen, Robert was sitting in the chair, waiting. "Are you okay?" he asked.

"No, I'm not okay. I ask you to leave now. Get out!" I yelled.

"Not until I know you're okay," Robert said.

"I either have a bug or I've eaten something rotten. That's all. Please go. I'm going to lie down." I said. "Please just leave. Joe will be here shortly, and I don't want to deal with anything right now."

"Okay, I'm going. I didn't mean to upset you," Robert said.

"If you didn't mean too, you wouldn't have come by. Please don't come again," I told him.

As Robert was getting into his car, Joe pulled up on his Harley. When he came in, he asked, "Are you okay? Robert said you were sick."

"I'm fine. Just morning sickness. I told him I had a bug or ate something rotten. I saw Shelly last night. Apparently, she and Robert are dating, so he came by to clear the air, but he said that it's not serious, but Shelly thinks it is. I can't get involved, though. They will have to figure this out themselves."

Joe asked, "Are you sure you don't want to tell him about the baby? If he's living here, it's bound to come out that you're pregnant. Will he suspect that it's his baby when he finds out?"

"I don't know, and I really don't care. I have too much to worry about without adding Robert into the mix. We can go to Florida for a long visit—just get away and relax. What do you think?" I asked.

"I would miss you both very much," Joe said quietly.

"I was talking about you going with us, silly."

"Okay, I think that might be a good idea. When do you want to go?" Joe asked.

"Let's leave in two weeks and stay all of August and September. What do you think?"

"I think it's a great idea. Let's get busy and start making plans," Joey said.

We made plans and worked out all the details. When Nicky came home, we told him that we were going to Florida, and that we were going to Disneyland. Nicky was super excited, and as the day went on, I felt better. We went shopping, and we went out for dinner. We went to Rosie's Italian restaurant, and after we got seated and turned our orders in, I excused myself and went to the ladies' room. I ran into Shelly there, and as soon as I said "Hi," Shelly burst into tears.

"Oh Shelly! What's the matter?" I asked.

"Robert broke up with me because of you," Shelly said. "He said that you wanted him to break up with me, and then he told me that he didn't love me and that he only loved you."

"I'm so sorry, Shelly, but he said he wasn't in a serious relationship." I put my arms around Shelly. "I'm sorry he hurt you, but Robert doesn't know what love is. He's not in love with me or anybody else. He doesn't even understand what love is," I said.

Shelly pulled back. "I could have made him happy if it wasn't for you interfering," Shelly said, and she ran out of the ladies' room.

I went after her, but she ran out of the restaurant. I went back to the table, and I saw sitting there with Nicky and Joe was Robert.

I walked over and asked, "Are you happy now that you hurt Shelly and blamed me for it? You need to grow up, Robert! You don't know what love is, and I'm glad you're out of my life. Now if you will excuse us, we'd like to enjoy our dinner without you."

Robert got up and walked away, but by the look he gave me, you could see the rage in his eyes. We had a quiet dinner. No one spoke at all, not even Nicky who usually talked nonstop, and then we went home in silence and Nicky fell asleep, so Joe carried him up to his room.

When Joe came downstairs, he said, "We need to talk." We went into the living room, and Joe said, "I love you, Missy, but I don't want to be your second choice, and if you can't say that you love me, then I think we need to just stay friends so that neither one of us hurts each other."

I looked up at Joe and said, "Joe, I care about you, but I'm not able to say that I love you. You mean the world to me and Nicky, but I'm not ready, and I'm not sure that I ever will be."

Joe smiled and walked over, and he kissed me on top of my head and said good night and left. I just sat on the couch and wasn't sure what to do or what to think. After sitting there for over an hour, I went to check on Nicky and then went to bed myself.

I slept really nicely, considering the kind of evening that I had, so I got up and showered and dressed.

I checked on Nicky, and he was still asleep, so I went downstairs and made coffee and breakfast. Nicky must have smelled bacon cooking because he came down in his pajamas to eat. As we sat at the table and ate, I told Nicky that we were going to Florida and it would be just the two of us. He asked about Joe, but I told him Joe couldn't get off work after all, so it would just be us, and he was okay with that. I made the reservations and booked several small trips and excursions to do while we were in Florida. I moved the trip up a week, and we packed everything that we needed, and anything else we forgot, we could just buy again if we need them. We went to the grocery and got snacks, travel games, and books for Nicky, and then I took the car to the dealership and had them change the oil and check everything so that we would be safe driving by ourselves. While they work on the car, we walked over to the pizza joint and ate lunch, and then we picked up the car and went home. When I pulled in, Joe was sitting on the front porch, and he came and helped with carrying everything in.

I thanked him for helping, and he said, "I had a call from Robert this morning."

I looked up. "Okay, what did he want?"

"He wants you back and said that he needs to make up for what happened."

I told Nicky to go watch TV, and then I looked at Joe and said, "That's his problem, not mine."

"Can you tell me exactly what happened between you two?" Joe said.

"No, I don't want to talk about it, and he could never make up for it, so there's no reason to discuss it."

"If I can help, I will. All you have to do is ask."

I smiled and said, "I'm a big girl. I can handle myself, and I can't give you what you deserve, so it's time I handle my life myself, but thank you, Joe. I never meant to take you for granted."

Joe smiled. "You didn't. We just fell into a routine, but I'll always be here as a friend if you need me," and he walked over, and we hugged.

"Thank you, Joe. You got me through when I needed you, but I'm fine now, and me and Nicky will be fine."

After Joe left, I called Shelly and asked her over, and she came by in the late afternoon. We talked about Robert and everything she needed to know to make her choice, and I told her me and Nicky was going on an extended vacation, but she could call me if she needed anything. After she left, I decided that maybe it was time to move somewhere else and start over.

I packed Nicky's clothes and the toys that he was taking on the trip, and I fixed him an overnight bag in case they stop over. Then I finished packing my bags. I cooked dinner, and after we ate, I let Nicky watch TV while I cleaned up the kitchen and took the trash out. Nicky helped me load the car, and Rachel and Matt came over and helped. Matt took Nicky to get ice-cream, and I fixed iced tea for me and Rachel. We sat on the front porch, and Rachel asked if everything was okay. I said mostly, and then I told Rachel everything—about what happened with me and Robert and Shelly; about how Joe and I are just friends since I couldn't commit because of the baby; and about my feelings over Robert. I told Rachel about my plans of moving and starting over. Rachel understood, but she told me that they would miss us dearly. I told her that I couldn't stay in the same town that Robert was in. He had no rights over me or the baby, and I planned on not telling him about the baby. Matt and Nicky came home, and we said our goodbyes, and I told Nicky to get ready for bed because we had to get up early and get on the road. Nicky came downstairs in his pajamas and gave me a kiss and hug good night, and then he went to bed.

I showered and put on my pajamas and went to bed. I slept until about six, and I got up and fixed egg and bacon sandwiches for the trip, and I had coffee and cereal before waking Nicky up. Once he was up, he ate his cereal and got dressed.

In the car, I got his seat buckled in with a pillow and a blanket, as well as his favorite stuffed bear that George gave him, and then we headed out to Florida.

Nicky fell asleep during the drive and woke up at around ten o'clock when I stopped to refill the gas and to get some coffee. Nicky was getting hungry, so I gave him his egg and bacon sandwich with soda, and we got back on the road.

We stopped at around two in the afternoon to refuel and eat lunch at Horn's, a café in Louisiana. The waitress was really nice and talked to Nicky like he was an adult. Then after our food came, the manager came over and asked if everything was good, so Nicky told him about us going to Disneyland and just talked his head off. I paid the waitress, and as we were leaving, the manager stopped us and gave Nicky a dozen of cookies for his trip. I thanked him, and we left.

We stopped overnight in lonesome Mississippi. We stayed at Holiday Inn, and I asked the night clerk why the town was called lonesome, She laughed and said it was supposed to be named twosome after the first mayor, but the guy who made all the signs and deeds at the bank couldn't read or write very well, so he misspelled the name on everything. The mayor thought it would be too much trouble to change everything, and he thought that it was funny.

I got Nicky settled in and ordered pizza for our dinner. After we ate, Nicky fell asleep in his clothes, so I just tucked him in bed and let him sleep. The next morning, after I showered, we had cold pizza for breakfast. Nicky showered and changed his clothes, and we got on the road. I stopped to refuel the car and got some coffee as we left the town and headed to Florida.

We drove again for several hours and made our stop in Dothan, Alabama, for gas refill and lunch. We went in a drive-through at McDonald's so that we could get to our condo unit before dinnertime. We seemed to be making a good time until we got on the Florida turnpike; we sat there for over two hours. Nicky was bored and hot, and when we finally got into Orlando, it was almost dark.

We got to the condo around ten that night, and I unloaded only what we needed. I planned to do the rest of the unloading in the morning. We had snacks, cereal but no milk, and canned tuna, which Nicky refused to eat, so we snacked on junk foods and soda instead and then went to bed.

I woke up around nine in the morning and checked on Nicky, but he was still sleeping, so I unloaded the car and put everything away, except our clothes. When Nicky came in crying, I picked him up and asked him, "What's the matter? We're finally here in Florida. Aren't you excited about going to Disneyland?"

Nicky looked up and said, "I miss George. He promised that he would take me to see Mickey Mouse."

I said, "I know he promised, but remember he had to go to heaven to be with his wife, Sophie, so he left that to me to do. Okay?" And I hugged him and realized how much we missed and depended on George.

Nicky said, "Okay, but I still miss him."

"I know you do, and so do I, but we have each other," I said.

Nicky looked up and said, "We have our baby too, Mommy. Don't forget about our baby."

I looked surprise and then smiled. "I won't forget about our baby, I promise. Now let's get washed up and dressed and go exploring, okay?" I told Nicky about the baby driving yesterday when he said that he would miss his friends.

We spent the day exploring Orlando and went on grocery shopping. Then after we got the groceries, we put them away and went out to lunch at Crusty Crab, a buffet restaurant with seafood and American food. They had girls dressed up as mermaids, and the waitresses and waiters wore pirate outfits. Nicky had his picture taken with them. He had a good time. Then we drove back to the condo and went swimming. On the way back to the condo, we decided to walk, and we saw an alligator in the creek between our condo and the general store. It came out of the water toward us, so we ran into the store. The clerk said the alligators are harmless, but I won't take any chances, so we called the security, and they took us to our condo. We also called the game warden to come and get the alligator.

We rested and took it easy the rest of the night, and Nicky went to bed early so that he could get up early we could go to Disneyland. I checked on Nicky who was fast asleep, and then I took a hot shower and went to bed. I had a headache, and my back was hurting, but I slept most of the night. The following day, we woke up early, had our breakfast, and went to Magic Kingdom. I bought five-day hoppers, and we spent most of the day in Magic Kingdom. By five o'clock in the afternoon, I got really tired, and my back was hurting. I wanted to go back to the condo, but Nicky wanted to stay for the fireworks. I checked on dinner at the castle, and they had a cancellation, so we only had to wait for an hour. Then we dined with Mickey, Minnie, Donald, and Daisy. Cinderella and Snow White made an appearance too. Dessert was served by Alice in Wonderland with the White Rabbit and Cheshire Cat and Mad Hatter. It was a wonderful night. Then as we came out of the castle, the fireworks started. Nicky was so excited, but then I suddenly felt sick and light-headed. A gentleman asked if I was all right. I told him I was not feeling well, and the next thing I knew, I was lying on the concrete ground with emergency workers over me.

"Where is Nicky?" I said over and over. The gentleman who asked me if I was okay was standing to the side holding Nicky, and Nicky was crying. I tried to get up, but the EMTs told me to lie still and that they were transporting me to the county. I told them I was fine and Nicky needed me. The EMT woman said that she was afraid that I had a miscarriage and that she would bring Nicky with her.

The night seemed to last forever. I was awake and sleeping on and off all night. I was woken up around ten the next morning by a doctor. "Ms. Chambers, I'm Dr. Todd. I need to ask you some questions. Are you up to talk?"

I looked up and asked, "Where's Nicky? Where's my son?"

Dr. Todd said, "Nicky's fine. He's out in the waiting room playing Nintendo with one of our nurses. He's been in here checking on you, and he slept in the doctor's lounge most of the night, so he's just fine, concerned about you." I was feeling sore and nauseous, but I sat up on bed. Dr. Todd asked, "Is this the first time you've had pain and sickness with this pregnancy?"

I answered, "I've had a headache and backache for about a week before we traveled here, and it's been constant since we got here."

Dr. Todd asked, "Did you have any problems with your first pregnancy?"

I said, "This is my first pregnancy. Nicky is my half brother. My dad passed away when he was three, and I've had him ever since."

Dr. Todd started to ask another question when I asked, "Did I lose my baby?"

Dr. Todd said, "No, but you're blood pressure is high, and toxemia has started to set in, so you're on complete bed rest until further notice. I'll have Connie bring Nicky in to see you."

I said, "Thank you, Doctor. Do I know you? You look familiar."

Dr. Todd said, "No, you don't know me, but I was there when you went down last night at the fireworks. I asked if you were okay, and then down you went. I called for help and kept Nicky for you."

I remembered seeing him hold Nicky. I smiled and said, "Thank you, Dr. Todd."

"If you want to thank me, you get better soon and don't scare me and Nicky again, okay?" Dr. Todd said and walked out.

The nurse brought Nicky in to see me, and he stayed until after lunch. Dr. Todd came in and checked on me, and he also talked to Nicky, and they played a video game. I thanked him and told him that he didn't have to entertain Nicky because I knew he must be busy, but he told me that he was on vacation on that week, and he just wanted to check on the little man. He stayed through most of the afternoon. I dozed off, and when I woke up, I saw him and Nicky eating pizza. I asked when I could go home, and Dr. Todd said that he would check with the on-call physician and left. The nurse came in and took my blood pressure again.

Dr. Todd came back and said, "You can go home as long as you stayed on bed rest for at least two weeks."

I told him that I would, and they started the paperwork. The nurse said that I could call my husband anytime to pick me up. I said okay, but I didn't tell her that I was actually single and that I couldn't go on bed rest because I had a four-year-old to take care of. They brought my papers in, and I signed them, and Dr. Todd came in with a wheelchair for me. I told him that I can walk, but he said, "Bed rest," and he proceeded to take me out to catch my ride.

I told Dr. Todd that I needed to call a cab, but he said that he was giving me a ride home. That way, I didn't have to cause inconvenience to anyone since he was available. I thanked him, and then he helped buckle Nicky in and helped him in the front seat of his SUV. I gave Dr. Todd the address of the condo, but he said, as we pulled out on the road, that he thought that maybe we should come home with him since there was no one to help me and Nicky. I told him that I would hire some help, but he said his mother insisted to bring us home and she would help take care of me and Nicky. I told him that I didn't want to bother anyone, but he said his mom had everything already set. We drove out of the city to the countryside, and I dozed off. I woke up when we turned into a driveway. It was beautiful; there was a tree-lined driveway and a white cottage on a sandy beach. There were palm trees and beautiful flowers everywhere.

Dr. Todd pulled up to the front of the cottage. A sweet older woman came out, smiling. Dr. Todd got Nicky out and then came around to my side, but I said, "Thank you, Dr. Todd, but I'm able of getting out of the car by myself."

He smiled and said, "Okay, I just wanted to help, and you can call me Todd instead of Dr. Todd. It's my first name. Most nurses and patients call me that because they have trouble with my last name."

I smiled. "What's your last name? Jesus?"

Todd laughed. "No, it's Heaven."

I laughed too. "Are you serious?"

He said, "Yes, I am. You can ask my mom."

Todd helped me out of the front seat and introduced me to his mom. "Mom, this is Melissa and little man Nicky. Melissa, this is my mom, Heather Heaven, and she likes to be called Heather."

Heather said, "It's so nice to meet you! I'm happy to have you stay with me 'til you're feeling better. I get lonely sometimes, and I get excited to have visitors."

Todd and Heather got Nicky and me settled in. Heather told me to rest while she fixed lunch, and she asked Nicky to help her, so off they went. Todd asked if I needed anything, and I said no. Then I remembered that we didn't have any clothes with us, but Todd said that we didn't need to worry. There were all kinds of clothes in their house from his sisters and his nephews. They would do until I feel better. I lay down to rest and fell asleep. I woke up after five o' clock in the afternoon. When I got up, I washed my face and went to find Nicky and Heather. They were in the kitchen: Heather was cooking dinner, and Nicky was cutting out cookies to bake.

Heather saw me and said, "Have a seat, dearie, and I'll get you some sweet tea."

Nicky said, "Look, Mommy, I'm making you cookies." And he ran over and hugged me.

"I bet they're the best cookies I'll have ever tasted," I told him. "Where's Todd at? I wanted to thank you and him for your hospitality."

Heather said, "He's gone home, but he'll be back for dinner."

"I thought he lived with you," Missy said.

"No, he has a fancy beach cottage about half a mile down the beach. He went home so that he wouldn't cramp your style, he said." Heather laughed.

I offered to help with dinner, but Heather refused. I was on bed rest, so she told me to put some clothes in her room in case I wanted to wash up and change and then I could curl up on the couch and relax. So I went and took a quick shower and changed into a light-blue sundress. Then I went on the deck and sat on the swing, watching the waves in the ocean. Todd came out to call me for dinner. He was dressed in a lavender shirt and purple shorts, and my heart almost stopped beating upon seeing him. I didn't realize how handsome he was, and it made me irritated that he was affecting me this way. You would think that I had learned my lesson that just because a man is handsome doesn't mean squat. It seemed like my mind didn't want to let this go. It must be the hormones because I was thinking about how he would look and feel with no clothes on. His eyes were dark smoky brown, and it was like I could see pain in them. The last time I felt this was with John. I liked Robert and Joe, but I didn't feel any connection to them. Maybe I'm just fickle. It seemed that every time I got interested in a man, they always let me down, and it ends in disaster. I had better keep my distance; he probably has a wife or a girlfriend.

The dinner was really good. Heather was a great cook, and Nicky's cookies were also great. During dinner, I asked Todd if he had a wife, but he said no, he never found the right woman yet. We talked about our trip to Disney and why Nicky and I were in Florida. Nicky told Todd about George. During dessert, we had coffee and coconut pie. Then after our dinner, I was getting really tired.

Todd said, "I need to take your blood pressure." His touch sent ripples through me. Afterward, he insisted that I go lie down since my blood pressure was up, and if I didn't want to go back to the hospital, I better had to rest. So I did.

I went straight to sleep. I woke up around midnight and got up to go to the restroom. But I tripped over someone's feet and fell into the small couch in the room. I landed on top of Todd. Todd caught me and asked, "Are you okay?"

I answered, "I'm fine. Why you are asleep in my room?"

Todd said, "I was worried about your blood pressure being so high, and you seemed restless, so I sat on the couch and fell asleep. Are you sure you're okay?"

"I'm fine," I said. "It's you I need to be asking. I fell on top of you. I could have hurt you." Then I burst out laughing.

Todd started laughing too. "I'm fine. You're the one who hardly weighs anything."

"I had better make a trip to the restroom, or you're not going to be fine," I said.

Todd helped me up, and when I came back, he had turned the light on and gotten the blood pressure cuff out waiting. My blood pressure was down, so he told me he would check on me again in the morning. Then he

"Todd, wait!" I said before he went out. "Instead of taking care of me while you're on vacation, why don't you go spend time with your girlfriend or buddies? I don't want to ruin your vacation."

Todd turned and looked at me and said, "I don't have time for a girlfriend, and I'm happy helping take care of you. I've had a rough month, and I feel better being here with you and Nicky." Then he left.

I went back to sleep and woke up early. I went to check on Nicky, but his bed was empty. So I went to the kitchen, and I saw Heather preparing breakfast. I took a cup of coffee and asked where Nicky was.

"He's on the beach with Todd, I hope that's okay. If you look out on the deck, you can see them playing," Heather said.

I walked over to the deck and saw them playing Frisbee. I went back to the kitchen and offered to help. Heather gave me some fruit to slice up to go with breakfast.

"They're having a good time," I said.

Heather said, "Good. Todd needs to relax and have some downtime. I'm glad you two are here."

I said, "I'm glad too, and I know Nicky is. Todd said last night that he had a rough month. Is there anything I can do? He's really gone out of his way to help me and Nicky."

"There's nothing anyone can do," Heather said. "Being a doctor, it's hard losing a patient. But he lost his best friend, his wife, and their young son in a car accident. And Todd was on duty that night. He took it really hard. He threw himself into his work trying to save everybody, and the hospital told him he needed time off to grieve and deal with the loss."

I was almost in tears. "I can't imagine how he must feel. I wish I could help."

Heather said, "You being here is helping him. Just be there if he wants to talk. But also enjoy life while you can because tomorrow can be gone in an instant."

We had a good time every time we had breakfast. Todd also checked my blood pressure several times a day that week. We got into a routine, and I felt like I'm almost home. I could tell that Nicky and I were getting close to Heather and Todd, and it was like we all fit together.

The days went into a week, and I thought that maybe I'd like living in this place. It's beautiful, and Heather and Todd were both great. Nicky and Todd were out on the beach again. They came in laughing and having a good time. Nicky told me about playing Frisbee and that they also built a sand castle. He also asked if it's okay that they go swimming later that day.

After breakfast, Todd took my blood pressure, and it was good. He said that if I wanted to get out, he would take me to the town market, and we could do lunch out. Then when we come back, he would take Nicky for a swim. I thanked him. It was good to get out after being on bed rest for a week. Each day, I kept on feeling better. At breakfast, I thanked Todd for taking me out. But I was worried since Nicky had never been in the ocean before. Todd told me that he was taking him to swim at his cottage and that he has an in-ground pool. I was cool with that.

After breakfast, I changed into a pink sundress, and Heather kept Nicky while Todd and I were gone. We drove into a small town where there were several stores, restaurants, and an outside market that had clothes, jewelries, fruits, and knick-knacks. I had a good time. We ate tacos and had margaritas then headed home. I was so happy without realizing that I was holding Todd's hand while we were walking from shop to shop.

Todd helped me into the car, and he leaned over to kiss me gently on the lips. Then he got into the car, and we drove home. The ride home was quiet, and I realized that I had fallen for Todd.

Maybe it was his kindness. How could I feel this way? When did it happen? Maybe I'm just confused because he was so sweet and kind. I was afraid to look at Todd, afraid that he would see what I was feeling for him. I had a baby on the way, Robert's baby. I didn't know what to do or think. He had never asked about the baby or the baby's father. Maybe he didn't even feel anything for me. Maybe it was just my imagination taking over.

When we pulled up to the cottage, I hopped out and ran inside to the bathroom.

Todd knocked on the door. "Are you okay?"

I was almost in tears. "I'm fine. Just had to go is all. Be out in a minute."

When I came out, they were in the kitchen, so I walked in, and Nicky asked, "It's my turn now, Mommy. Can I go swimming now?"

I looked at Todd, and he said, "I'm ready if you're ready." Then Todd asked me, "Want to come along?"

"I'm tired. I think I might lie down for a nap," I said.

Todd said okay, and they left to go swimming.

Heather asked if I had a good time, and we talked about all the shops, and I showed her a pin that I bought for her as a thank-you gift for taking us in. After I drank my iced tea, I went and lay down.

As I lay there, it seemed like I had been there forever, and I didn't want to leave, but I must get the strength to go. I had the condo for a few more days, and then we were supposed to go to George's house to stay until I decided what to do. I looked up the address of George's house, and it was just about twenty minutes away from Heather's house, just on the other side of town.

When it was time for dinner, I asked Todd if he could ride me over to the house to check it out. It had innkeepers on the ground, so I could call them, and he said, "I'll take you over tomorrow. I took you out earlier today. I don't want you to overdo it."

After dinner, it got cloudy, and a storm blew up really quick. Heather said that it was normal. It usually rained ten times a week and was sunny in between the rains and storms. The storms weren't from a hurricane, even though it was hurricane season. The storm blew over around midnight.

The next morning, I called the Millers and let them know I was coming by to check out the house, and they said they would unlock the house and air it out. After breakfast, Heather kept Nicky, and Todd took me to the house.

It was about twenty minutes past the town that we went to yesterday. It was a two-story cottage with a long driveway, big front porch and a deck, an in-ground pool, and a hot tub, and it was about two miles off a private beach. It also had a huge garage and an office and sunroom. There was a pickup truck, SUV, and sports car parked in the garage. There were five bedrooms, all with their own bathrooms, plus a half bath on the first floor. It was a really nice big house and was fully furnished. It had pictures of George, Sophie, and James, their son, on the walls. There was also a black baby grand piano in the living room. Looking at the family pictures, you could tell how happy they were.

Todd asked, "Can you be happy here in Florida?"

I smiled. "Yes, I can be happy here. I love the weather, the land, and the people here."

Todd smiled too. "You must have loved George and his family very much. You look so content looking at the pictures. And how are you related?"

I told Todd how I met George and how we became family and everything in between. We talked all afternoon, and when it was time to leave, Todd asked, "What about the baby's father? Is he in the picture? Is he in your life?"

"No, he's not. This baby was conceived in a one-night stand, and he doesn't know and never will," I said.

Todd said, "I'm not judging, I just want to know where I stand in this relationship. You see, I think I'm falling in love with you, and I hope you feel the same."

I looked at Todd and said, "My life is messy and out of control, and I think I love you too. But I just don't want to rush it. Is that okay? Can we take it slow?"

Todd smiled. "We can. Take it slow as a snail if that's what you want." And he leaned over and kissed me, gently at first then more passionately.

We went and had lunch, then went back to Heather's house to check on them. When we pulled up, there were police cars, a fire truck, and an ambulance. Todd barely had the truck stopped as we hopped out and went running in the house. Nicky was crying, and a policeman was holding him, and in the living room were the EMTs and several firemen working on Heather. I took Nicky and held him, and Todd was over by Heather, talking to her, telling her that he loved her and that she needed to hang on.

After what seemed like a lifetime, they had Heather on the stretcher and loaded her in the ambulance. Todd came over and asked Nicky if he was okay, and he said yes. He tried to help Heather, and Todd gave him a hug and kiss and said he was riding in the ambulance with her. I told him I would be at the hospital as soon as I could get there, and he kissed me. He went and got in with Heather.

The policeman said that Nicky called for help, and he stayed on the phone until they got there. He also told Nicky that he was a hero and was proud of him for saving Heather and that he didn't panic at all. He told me to follow him to the hospital, so we did.

When we got to the hospital, they had Heather in a room, and Todd was in the waiting room. The policeman that I followed came in and asked

Nicky if he was hungry. Of course, Nicky said yes, so he asked if he could take Nicky to the cafeteria. I smiled and said thank you.

I asked Todd, "Have you heard anything about Heather?"

"Heather had a heart attack, and if it wasn't for Nicky, she wouldn't have made it here," he said. You could tell how upset he was.

I asked, "Has the doctor been out to talk to you?"

Todd said, "Not yet."

And just then, the doctor came out and told Todd, "Heather had a massive heart attack. There was a lot of damage. Once we get her stable, I'm going in to repair her heart muscle and probably put in a pacemaker. But she's awake, and she's asking for you and Missy." He cautioned us not to stay too long.

We were waiting on a bed in ICU. We stayed until they got Heather in her room. Nicky wanted to see her, but I told him he would have to wait until she was in a regular room. But Todd said that he saved Heather, so he should see her to know that she was okay. He warned him about all the machines and tubes and told him to try not to be afraid that she needed everything in there to help her get better. Nicky said that he would be brave, so he went to see Heather. Then Todd came out to get me and Nicky. Nicky was so brave; Heather was thanking him for saving her.

"I love you, Heather! I don't want to lose you. I'll always take care of you," Nicky said. And Todd picked Nicky up and lifted him over to Heather. He gently kissed Heather and whispered, "I love you."

Heather told Nicky, "I love you too, and I'll be home in no time, I promise."

Then I also blew kisses to Heather and told her I would see her again later. I took Nicky out to the waiting room and sat down. Nicky crawled in my lap and asked, "Is Heather going to heaven to be with George and Sophie?"

I smiled and said, "I don't think so, honey, but we need to say our prayers for her when we get home." And I gave him a big hug and kiss.

Nicky fell asleep in my lap, and Todd came out and said it was time to go home. I offered to stay the night with Heather and he could take Nicky home so they could rest, but he said that Heather told him to take us home and get some rest. So Todd carried Nicky to the SUV and buckled him in, and we drove home in silence.

When we got to Heather's house, Todd carried Nicky and put him to bed, and then I made hot tea and fixed sandwiches. We sat at the kitchen table, eating in silence.

I looked over at Todd and asked, "Are you okay? Can I do anything for you?"

Todd smiled and said, "You could hold me just for a while, and then you can go to bed and get some rest."

I walked over to Todd and put my arms around him, and he put his arms around me. He just held me for the longest time, and then he looked up at me and smiled. "You'd better get some sleep." He kissed me, and I said, "Why don't you come and lie down with me, and I'll hold you all night?"

Todd asked, "Are you sure?"

"I'm very sure," I said and took Todd's hand, and we walked down the hall. I peeked in on Nicky, and he was sound asleep, so we went into my room, and I smiled. "Now lie down, and I'll hold you as long as you want me to."

Todd reached for me and pulled me in his arms. He kissed me gently at first and then with more passion. We lay down in bed, and Todd slowly made passionate love to me over and over until we fell asleep.

We woke up at around seven the next morning. I hopped out of bed and turned the alarm off. Todd never moved. He was so exhausted from the day before. I hopped in the shower and got dressed. Todd was still sleeping, so I checked on Nicky, who was also sleeping. I went in the kitchen and made coffee, fried the bacon, and sliced up the tomatoes when I heard Todd behind me.

"Good morning! I was trying not to wake you. I know you're exhausted and could use some more sleep."

Todd smiled. "I'm fine. I need to get to the hospital and check on Heather."

I served him coffee and bacon and tomato sandwich.

"Why do you call your mom by her given name?" I asked.

Todd smiled and said, "Mom and Dad were hippies, and that's what I was taught to call them. It was always Bill and Heather. It was just the way they did things."

"Really, are you pulling my leg?" I said.

Todd said, "I might later tonight, but I'm telling you the honest truth." Then he laughed.

Nicky came into the kitchen and asked when we were going to the hospital, but Todd said, "You're staying home today, you and your mom, but I'll be back to check on you two later this afternoon." He put his cup and plate in the sink and kissed Nicky on the head and whispered, "I love you, buddy."

Nicky smiled and said, "Me too. Will you tell Heather that I love her and miss her?"

Todd said, "Yes, I will." Then he walked over to me and kissed me and said, "I'll call you later," and left.

I cleaned the house and cooked dinner early in case Todd came home hungry. Nicky helped me all day. We cleaned Heather's bedroom, and we stripped her bed to wash her sheets. Her mattress was in really bad shape, so I called the furniture store and ordered Heather an adjustable bed and new mattress. Then I called the general store and asked about sheets and bedding. Tabatha the girl at the store sent me pictures of beddings, and I ordered two sets of sheets, one that was light blue with white roses on them, with matching blanket and quilt, and a second set of light pink with tropic flowers and another matching blanket. The saleslady said she would bring them out later that day, and the bed would arrive the following day. So when Heather comes home, she would be comfortable.

Todd called late afternoon and said Heather was doing great. The doctors said they were doing her surgery in two days, but they were pleased that she was feeling better. They were currently doing the test and the surgery the next day. He said he was coming home for a couple of hours, and if we felt like it, we could go see Heather this evening.

Todd got home around four in the afternoon, and he looked so tired. He sat down, and I prepared him a plate of food, as well as Nicky. Todd told us what all the doctors had said, and after her surgery, they would set up rehab at home. They would order her a hospital bed and everything she needed, but she couldn't be by herself until she was totally healed.

Nicky was so excited that he told Todd about the bed and bedding we ordered and that he couldn't wait until he saw Heather tonight so that he could tell her. Todd thanked us but said that we didn't have to do that; he could afford a bed and sheets. Then he walked and went out on the deck.

Nicky asked, "Is he mad at us, Mommy?"

"No, he's just tired and upset about his mom, that's all," I said.

Nicky finished eating and went out to see Todd. I cleaned up the dishes and put the food away. Todd and Nicky came in.

Todd walked over and said, "I'm sorry about earlier. I don't know why I acted that way. Forgive me, please."

I turned around and said, "Of course, I forgive you. I was only trying to help, but if I overstepped, just let me know." I put my arms around him and kissed him.

Todd smiled and said, "You didn't. I'm just really tired, and I'm worried about her. She seems like she is trying too hard to make everybody believe she's feeling better."

They got ready to leave for the hospital when my phone rang; it was Robert. I hit silence, and we left. The phone rang again several more times, and it was still Robert. I finally answered the phone, and Robert said, "About time. Too busy whoring around to answer?"

"What I do and with who is none of your concern. What do you want?" I asked.

"Sorry for bothering you. I just wanted to tell you about Shelly," Robert said.

"What about Shelly? What did you do now?" I asked.

"She's pregnant, and we're getting married. Thought you might want to know," Robert said.

"Congratulations! I'm happy for her, and I hope you treat her right," I told him.

Robert started to say something when I hung up.

Todd asked if everything was okay, and I told him, "A friend of mine is having a baby with a jerk, and I wish her luck."

The rest of the trip to the hospital was quiet. Nicky was so excited to see Heather and the nurse that helped him on the day we brought Heather to the hospital. When we arrived, the nurse was working, and she asked Nicky if he wanted to go to dinner with her. Nicky asked me if he could go, and I said yes. We could tell by the way the nurse was acting that something was wrong, so we went to the ICU and found out that Heather had another heart attack just before we got there, and the doctors were in her room. The doctors explained that they couldn't wait for two days for the surgery. They had kept Heather stable now, but they didn't know for how long. They would take her to surgery at six in the morning.

You could tell that Todd was worried, so we stayed in Heather's room after the doctors left. They had her hooked up to a lot of monitors than she had last night, and they had IVs in both arms. The nurse said that they were doing a port first before surgery and that instead of a pacemaker, they were putting in a defibrillator.

Heather was weak, and her voice was shaky, but she told Todd that she loved him and that she was so very proud of everything he had done and accomplished in his life. She also said that he needs to find love and joy and that he deserves to be happy. Then she looked at me and said, "Missy can make you happy. I know you love her and Nicky, and you will love this new baby also."

Then she asked if she could see Nicky before we left, but Todd said he was staying the night, and I also said I wasn't leaving and the nurses would help us with Nicky. But Heather said that Nicky didn't need to be there all night, so I told her we would figure something out.

Todd went out, and I sat with Heather all evening. The nurse and Todd came in with Nicky, but Heather was sleeping, so Nicky sat in my lap and waited until she woke up. Sherry the nurse asked if she could take Nicky home with her when she got off work, and she would bring him back tomorrow afternoon since it was her day off. She really wanted to help out.

Todd said that Sherry is an experienced babysitter and that Nicky would be in good hands, so I agreed. Sherry sat with me and Nicky while Todd was in with Heather. She was really nice. She had known Heather and Todd for years and was a close family friend, which made me feel better. Nicky really liked Sherry, but Nicky wouldn't leave until he saw Heather and talked to her. So we sat in the waiting area, and Sherry gave Nicky paper and crayons so that he could draw Heather a picture. When Heather woke up, she asked Todd to see Nicky and insisted that he picked him up and put him beside her. I said that it wasn't a good idea, but Heather said it was all right, so Todd put Nicky up beside Heather, and they talked so low, it was almost like a whisper. Nicky carefully kissed Heather and gave her a small gentle hug before he got ready to leave. Then he told Heather that he would take care of everything, and Sherry reminded him to kiss me and Todd and told him that he would see us tomorrow. Then they left.

We stayed in the ICU waiting room most of the night, going back and forth. Then we got in her room early so that the doctor could talk with us. They took her at 5:00 a.m., and we said our goodbyes and told her we loved her. I gave her a hug and whispered that we need her in our lives, so she should hang in there. The nurse came out around seven to say that they put the port in and had no problems and that they were preparing to start the other procedure. The surgery took all day, and we got updates every now and then. Afterward, the nurse came over and said that she was in recovery and the doctors would be out soon. The doctors were really happy that everything went smooth. They had Heather in her room by five o'clock in the afternoon, and we sat with her for a while. Sherry brought Nicky so he could see us, and he asked about Heather, but we told him he couldn't see her for few days. He stayed with us for about an hour, and he said Sherry was taking him to Rocket Time Pizza. We took turns going in to check on Heather, and Sherry came back around dinnertime and brought us fast-food meal and took Nicky out for pizza with her nephews. She kept him for another night and said that she would bring Nicky back as soon as she came to work tomorrow evening.

After we ate, the nurse asked us to come sit with Heather. She was awake, and they had taken her off the ventilator. She was having trouble talking, but she looked good, and we told her not to talk since we just wanted to sit with her.

The doctor came in before eleven o'clock and said that she was fine. We can go home to get some sleep since Heather was doing great. He said that she would sleep all night because of the medicines, and other than waking up for a few minutes on and off, she would just drift off to sleep again. Todd kissed Heather on her cheek, and she smiled and whispered hoarsely good night. Then we went home. I fixed Todd a sandwich and an iced tea, but he said he was too tired to eat, so we went to bed. When I came out of the bathroom, he was sound asleep on the bed, so I crawled in beside him and fell asleep instantly. I woke up around five that morning, cramping, and even though I was scared, I didn't tell Todd. I didn't want to put any more stress on him. I took a relaxing bath, and the cramps seemed to ease up. After drying off, I went ahead and got dressed, and then I called the nurses station to check on Heather. The night nurse said that she was having a good and restful night but that she had to go for an MRI at eight in the morning, and the doctor would be in to see her. I made coffee, and I heard Todd behind me. I turned around, and he encircled me in his arms and kissed me. He smiled and said, "Thanks for letting me sleep, but I need to get to the hospital to check on Heather."

I smiled. "I just talked to the nurse. She's had a good night. But they're taking her down for an MRI at eight. Then the doctor will be in."

"I had better get dressed. I thought I had more time, but maybe tonight we can enjoy each other," Todd said.

I blushed, and Todd went to get dressed. I was still cramping, but I didn't say anything. We drove to the hospital, and the doctor was just bringing Heather back from X-ray. The doctor came in later that morning and said that everything looked good and that if she kept improving in a couple of days, they would transfer her to PCU. After the doctor left, I told Todd that I was going to make phone calls and I'd be back later. I kissed him and winked to Heather. I walked down to the ER and asked to be examined. I told the nurse that I was almost six months pregnant with cramping and spotting. They took me straight back and called the ob-gyn. I told him about my blood pressure, and that was probably it. But I wanted to make sure, so the nurse help me into a gown, and the doctor examined me, and they did an ultrasound. My blood pressure was high, and I had some swelling, so he ordered medicine and advised bed rest. The doctor wanted to admit me, but I told him I couldn't. I also told him about Todd, Heather, and Nicky, so he agreed to me putting my feet up and taking the medicine, but if my cramps came back, I needed to come back to the ER, and they would admit me. He said that I needed to take care of myself and my baby girl. I hadn't thought about the baby's gender with everything going on, but now that I know, I had better start planning for my daughter. I couldn't wait to tell Todd and Nicky, but I couldn't say anything now because Todd would know that I had been to the ER. The doctor said that he would make sure that I had a recliner to sit in and that I needed to put my feet up, so I told him I would and went and got coffee from the cafeteria for Todd. Then I went to the ICU. As I came through the double doors, the nurse in charge said that they would bring me up a recliner and that I needed to come to the front desk every two hours for the nurse to check my blood pressure. I told her thanks, but I didn't want to worry Todd or Heather, so she said they would be discreet. I brought Todd his coffee, and he seemed relieved that I was back. Todd kissed me and asked, "What took you so long? I thought maybe you had gone to the emergency room or something."

I was glad that Heather was sleeping. I gave Todd a big hug and smiled. I wanted to tell him about my baby girl, but I decided to wait.

"No, I just had phone calls, and I needed to call the furniture store, remember?" I said.

Todd looked surprised. "I forgot. Are they coming today?"

I answered, "No, I set it up for Monday. With it being Friday today, I didn't want to rush them, and I have another surprise. Robert, the owner of the general store, called, and he and his two boys are coming by tomorrow to paint Heather's bedroom before the bed comes."

Todd smiled. "That's why I love living here. It's like a family in our small town, and everyone helps each other. Heather will be so surprised. I promised that I would paint her house two years ago, but I was just so busy with work, but I realize that work isn't everything. Family and love is number 1. I owe that to you. I don't think I've ever been in love until I met you." And he came over to where I was sitting, put his arms around me, and kissed me.

The nurse came in with the recliner and said, "I thought this might be more comfortable since you're expecting. Don't forget to put your feet up. They look a little swollen. And if you need anything, just let me know." Then she left the room.

Todd looked at me and my ankles and said, "Yes, they are. You should have stayed home and rested today."

But I said, "I'm where I want to be." The nurse came in to check Heather's vitals. When she woke up, she reached for my hand, and I got up and went over and held her hand till she dropped back off. I took a rest on the chair with my feet up, and I got up to go to the restroom every two hours. The nurse took my blood pressure, and it was still high, but not as high as earlier. The nurse said that I needed to take my medicine again that Dr. Sheik gave me, but I forgot to get it filled, so the nurse called down and ordered it for me. When I went back in Heather's room, she was awake and talking. Todd excused himself, and I sat and talked with Heather until he came back. I told Heather that I was having a girl, and she got excited. But I told her that I was going to tell Todd and Nicky about it tomorrow, so she said that she wouldn't say a word. Todd came back with lunch; he had a cold Coke and a salad from the cafeteria and a cheeseburger and coffee for him. They started Heather on ice chips earlier in the day, and as long as she didn't get sick, she could have clear liquids for dinner. The nurse asked Todd to get some fresh ice chips for Heather, and when he left the room, she gave me my medicine. So I took a pill before Todd came back in. I slept on the chair, and my phone rang; it was Sherry. Her nephew was sick, and she had called in to let us know that she was keeping Nicky and her nephew separated, but she was keeping them again tonight. She then asked how I was feeling and if my blood pressure was down. I told her I was doing good. After I got off the phone, Todd said, "I heard Sherry asking about your blood pressure. With everything going on, we haven't check it. I'll go get the nurse to check it." And out he went. Not sure what to say, so I didn't say anything, and Todd had the nurse from the other side of the ICU to check my blood pressure. It was down, and the nurse asked if my medicine ever came up, and I said yes, thank you, and she left. Todd asked me what did she mean, and I told him that I had my medicine filled because I had left it at home and had forgotten to take it this morning. He didn't say anything else.

Heather suggested that we go home and get some rest, but we stayed another couple of hours. I was feeling back to normal, and I had the nurse checked my blood pressure again, and it was all the way down. The doctor came in after dinner to see how well Heather did on clear liquids and said he was impressed with how well she was responding. He told us we needed to get out and eat some good food and get some rest. We told Heather we would be back tomorrow, and we left. Todd asked if I want Italian food, and I said yes, and he took me to Emma's. It was a nice restaurant with family-style eating, and we went over the menu. We ordered spaghetti and meatballs with bread and salad. It was delicious. Todd ordered a piece of carrot cake to split, and then after dinner, we went home. Todd helped me get comfortable on the couch, and he prepared some iced tea for us as we watched the news. A tornado hit Pennsylvania and did a lot of damage in Pigeon Hollow, close to my hometown, so I called Margaret to check on them. They were hit hard; there was no electricity, the garage and back part of the house was in shambles, but other than a few cuts and bruises, everybody was fine. She put everyone in hotels, and tomorrow in the daylight, she would tell me more. I thanked her and told her to call me tomorrow. I told Todd about the house and that I would get more details tomorrow. Todd said that I needed to stay home tomorrow and rest, and I agreed, but I really wanted to check on Heather. So Todd said he would keep me updated. We got ready for bed, and Todd helped me. I told him that I was fine, and he said, "Dr. Shriek said you're to take it easy and take your medicine."

I looked up shock and said, "He told you. I told him that I didn't want to cause you any more stress than what you have now."

"I ran into Jim in the cafeteria, and he asked about Heather, and I told him how good she's doing. Then I asked him how he knew about her, and he said you told him. So I put two and two together, and he admitted it that you were in ER this morning," Todd said. "No matter what's going on, you can tell me anything, don't you know that?"

I smiled. "I was trying to protect you, but since I can tell you anything, I'm having a girl."

Todd smiled real big. "We're having a girl. We need to get busy and start fixing a nursery up for her." And he grabbed and hugged and kissed me, and passion started to rise, but Todd said, "Oh, no, you don't. You go to sleep, I'll sleep on the couch. You need to take it easy."

"We can be careful," I said, but Todd said, "No, not until I know you're back to normal and not having issues."

"Will you at least sleep with me and hold me? I'll behave I promise," I said, smiling.

Todd smiled and said, "You sleep, and I'll hold you all night. I love you, Missy."

"I love you too," I said. And we slept all night. The next day, Todd woke me up with breakfast in bed, and I told him, "I could get use to this, but I have work to do. Robert and his boys said they would be here around ten, so I need to clear your mom's room."

Todd said, "Already done. And Sherry is bringing Nicky home at lunchtime with lunch for you and the paint crew. I've asked her to check your BP and let me know what it is. I'm leaving for the hospital to check on Heather, and I'll be back early. Okay, love you, and call me if you need anything." He kissed me, and out the door he went.

I was preparing my coffee when I heard Robert and his boys pulling up. I offered them coffee and soft drinks, but Robert said they needed to get busy, so I stayed out of their way. And just before Sherry arrived, Robert and his boys came out and said they were finished with Heather's bedroom, and Robert wanted me to come check it out. I went in, and they had done an amazing job. They had painted the ceiling and trimmed everything in white, and the walls were a beautiful light blue. So when I went back into the kitchen, they had already moved the kitchen table and chairs outside and was moving the appliances out from the walls so that they could paint the kitchen. I said, "You don't have to paint the kitchen. I just wanted her bedroom done before she comes home."

Robert said, "We're painting the dining room, living room, hallway, and the bathroom."

I said, "That's too much for you to do!"

Charlie, Robert's oldest son, said, "Heather means the world to us, we want to do this. Why don't you go out to lunch and we'll do our work."

About that time, Sherry pulled up, and Raymond and Charlie went out to help her in. Nicky came running in and asked if his room was being painted, and I said, "No, but I'll help you clean it today."

Nicky said, "Shockey darn, I wanted my room blue like Heather's." We went to the living room, and Sherry gave the guys their food, and she came in and took my BP. It was good, so she told me to go get ready because we were going out to lunch.

I said, "I need to stay here in case Robert and the boys need anything."

Robert peak his head around the corner and said, "We're big boys. We can take care of ourselves"

Sherry said, "Thank you, Robert."

I started to say something, but Sherry said, "After lunch, I'm taking you to the hospital to see Todd and Heather. She's doing great, and maybe when we get there, she'll be in her regular PCU room. She's having a fit not seeing Nicky."

"I'm glad she's doing so good. Todd was really worried, and so was I," I said.

Sherry said, "She has the best doctor in his field, and he's really pleased with her recovery. Let's get some lunch, and you can see for yourself."

They ate at Sandy's Diner, and the food was excellent. Nicky even asked for dessert, so I let him have a cookie surprise, which turned out to be a huge sugar cookie with ice-cream cool whip and chocolate syrup. It took all three of us to eat it. Then we went to the little shop next door. Sherry said she needed to get a dress for a wedding, so we looked around and we saw beautiful dresses, mainly wedding and bridesmaid dresses, they also have flower and ring bearer clothes. I told Sherry I was having a girl, so we looked at the fancy dresses for babies. I found a beautiful wedding dress in the store that I fell in love with, but by the time I have a baby and get married, it would be gone. Sherry said that she wanted to put a dress on layaway, so I took Nicky to the car so she could take care of her business. We went to the hospital and Heather had been moved, and Nicky was so excited to see her. I warned him that she might be weak and that he needed to be careful to not cause any accident that might hurt her. When we went in her room, she was up in the recliner, eating lunch, and she looked great. I gave her a hug and kiss, and she told Nicky to hop up in the chair with her. I started to say that wasn't a good idea, but Todd smiled and said it was fine. And he came over to me, kissed me, and told me I needed to sit and relax. Sherry walked in with the nurse and brought another recliner so that I could put my feet up. I thanked them, and Sherry gave me a hug and said, "You have to take care of yourself. I'll check on you later. I'm going to get ready for work. Let me know if you all need anything." She left so she could get ready for her shift. Nicky and Heather were watching TV, and Todd said he would be back later. Before long, I had dozed off. Todd woke me when he came back, and I said, "I'm sorry, Heather. You're the one in the hospital, and I'm the one sleeping."

Heather said, "You go back to sleep. I just rang the nurse so that I can get in bed for a nap. Also, Todd, can you get Nicky? He fell asleep, and after they help me in bed, he can lie down with me and nap." The nurse came in and helped Heather in bed, and I had Todd put Nicky in my lap. He was just too heavy to hold at his age, and after Heather got situated, she told Todd to put Nicky in bed with her so that I could rest, and he did when he sat down. I told him I didn't want Nicky to wear Heather out, but he said that was the other way around. They napped through the afternoon and I told Todd to go get him something to eat and I'd watch over them. So he left, and I watched TV until they woke from their naps.

Heather said, "I'm so glad that you're having a girl. I'm so excited." And Nicky's eyes got big. He got excited and said, "You're having a baby girl? I'm going to be a big brother and have a sissy?"

Heather said, "Nicky, that's not nice." But I said, "It's okay, the neighbors had their grandkids a lot and they called her Sissy instead of her name Suzie."

Heather said, "You're going to be a great big brother to your Sissy." And Nicky grinned ear to ear. We talked about names, but I told her I hadn't thought about it yet. And she told me that I needed to start thinking about names and getting things for the baby. Todd walked in and he sat on the foot of the bed and talked with Nicky, and Nicky informed him that he was going to be a great big brother to his sissy and that he will help me get things for her, like toys and diapers. Nicky talked and laughed and I went to the restroom, and when I came back in, everyone was quiet. So I asked, "What did I miss?"

And Heather said, "Nothing, were just watching cartoons. It's starting to get dinner time, why don't you guys go home and get some rest?"

We stayed a while longer then we left, and Todd stopped at an Italian restaurant. We had a great dinner. Then I asked him why everyone was quiet when I came back, but he said it was nothing, then we headed home. It was dark when we got there, but the lights were on in the kitchen and living room. As we walked in the kitchen, Robert and his boys had done a great job. The kitchen was painted a light yellow, and they had put all the appliances back in place as if they were never moved. We looked in the dining room and it matched the kitchen. Then as we went into the living room, they had painted it a light lavender color, and it looked great. It went all the way down the hallway, and the bathroom was white trimmed in a teal color.

"I can't believe they did this all in one day," I said.

Todd said, "Robert use to have his own painting company and when wallpaper came out, his business got real slow, so he bought the general store. He paints on the side, and he does amazing work."

"Yes, he does," I said.

Nicky came out of his room excited. "My room is blue. Mommy, come see it." And we followed him. They really had painted his room the same as Heather's. Nicky kissed me goodnight and I asked Todd if he needed anything, and he said no he was fine. He's really tired so we got ready for bed. We made love several times that night and slept in each other's arms for the rest of the night.

I heard a truck the next morning, and it was Robert and his two boys. They came to finish painting Heather's house. Todd was already up and had let them in, and I got dressed and went to the kitchen. I smiled at Todd and walked over to him and kissed him. "Good morning, what's going on? I thought Robert and his guys were done."

Todd smiled. "They're finishing up today. I'm going to the hospital, but I plan on taking you and Nicky to my house for the day."

Nicky came in and said, "Yes, we can swim, Mommy."

I looked at Nicky and said, "I can't swim, so you can't swim today."

Todd smiled. "You can't swim? Didn't you have lessons when you were a kid?"

"No, my mom was sick and after she passed away, my father didn't really bother with me, so I never had the chance to learn," I said.

Todd said, "I'll teach you after Heather comes home, okay? But there's other things there, you'll find plenty to do there."

While Nicky packed a backpack with a few toys, I took a quick shower and got my laptop and paperwork to work on while Todd was at the hospital. The phone rang, and it was the girl from the general store. She said that they were bringing the bed and everything I ordered tomorrow and that she and her sister Carla was coming out to help me get Heather's bedroom done. So I thanked her and I told Todd. He said that would be great and that the doctor talked about sending Heather home by Tuesday or Wednesday. Todd dropped us off at his house. It was the first time I had been there so Nicky showed me the house and pool and Todd's beach. Nicky watched TV and I worked on my paper work and called Margaret to check on everything there. Margaret said the work was progressing and that they should be completed in two weeks. I asked her what she thought about selling the house, if she thought everyone would be okay with it, and she said that I didn't need to keep a house just because it was a house, that I needed to make a life for me and Nicky, and live where we would be happy. So I thanked her and told her I'd get back to her on my decision. It started raining so I watched a Disney movie with Nicky. Then we made lunch, and Nicky was playing with his toys while I washed up the dishes. And when I went to check on him, he was asleep in the recliner, so I lay on the couch for a nap also. Todd woke me around two in the afternoon and Nicky was watching cartoons.

Todd said, "Wake up, Sleeping Beauty!"

I smiled. "How's Heather today?"

"She's doing great there sending her home tomorrow afternoon after they run x-rays to make sure everything's fine," Todd said.

I smiled. "I'm glad. I know she'll be glad to be in her own bed." Then it darned on me that her bed wasn't coming until tomorrow. "Oh no! Her furniture isn't coming until the morning. Todd, can you take her out to lunch on the way so that we can get her room done? There bringing her bed between eight and twelve."

Todd said, "It will be okay; her x-rays aren't until eleven, so by the time I get her check out, you should have plenty of time."

I smiled. "I hope so she'll want to lay and take it easy, so I had better have her bed done by then." Then I asked, "Are we going to see her this afternoon? Is that why you're so early?"

Todd smiled. "No, Heather sent me home, said she was tired of me watching her, told me to come home and take you and Nicky out to eat. So that's why I'm here."

"That sounds good. Can we go by the house and check if Robert and his boys are done? I want to check to make sure I have enough cleaning supplies so that I can clean tonight, and then tomorrow I can do Heather's room," I said. We stopped by the cottage and Robert's truck was gone, so when we walked in the house, it was clean from top to bottom. They had painted the entire house, all the rooms was painted and trimmed out in white. And then they cleaned each room and put things back in place. There was a note, it read:

Missy,

We finish all we could do today but well be back in the morning to help you get Heather's room done.

Robert, Charlie, and Raymond

"That's so sweet of them, but they don't have to do it all. I'm quite capable of finishing the house," I said.

Todd smiled and said, "Yes you are, but you also have to take care of yourself. And anyway, Robert and Heather are close. After my dad passed away, Heather worked for Robert when he had his paint company and they developed a relationship after Sara, Robert's wife, passed away with cancer. The boys were only in their early teens, and Sara told the boys that Robert needed to go on with his life and find love. That's what god would want for him and you boys, so they were really happy about Heather and Robert. But Heather wouldn't commit until the boys graduated. And by then, it just remained the same. Robert would visit during the week when he had time, and Heather would go over there on the weekends until the last year. Heather wouldn't tell me why or what change, and Robert said he hadn't a clue as to why she quite coming over and making excuses when he called so that he wouldn't come over."

"I'm sorry, I didn't know," I said. "Do you think she might get upset that I had Robert paint?" I asked.

"No, I don't think so. He's been to the hospital to see her several times, and so had Raymond and Charlie. Maybe she'll wake up and realize that Robert loves her. Let's go eat, I'm starving," Todd said.

We went to the pizza shack for dinner and we all ate. Then Todd helped Nicky play video games in the arcade. After that, we stopped at the store and I picked up a few groceries and cleaning supplies. Then we went home. After we got back, Nicky took a bath and put his Star Wars pajamas on, and I tucked him in. He asked, "Is Heather coming home soon? I miss her."

"Hopefully tomorrow she'll come home. You better get some sleep, we have plenty of work to do in the morning so that we can get Heather's room ready for her. And I love you. Night," I said.

I gave him a kiss and went to find Todd. He was watching TV. I went and watched the news with him, then we went to bed. Todd made love to me on and off all night long and we slept in between. The alarm woke me at 6:00 a.m. and I got up, turned the alarm off, and showered and dressed in jeans and T-shirt. I started preparing coffee and heard the shower going, so I fried sausage and eggs for breakfast. Nicky woke up and had breakfast with us, then Robert and the box truck pulled in at nine, and behind the truck was Charlie, Raymond, and Sherry is in the pickup truck, and in the blue car is the girl from the general store, Tabatha and Crystal her sister. They unloaded the bed and Todd help Robert put it together, then Todd left for the hospital and he kissed me and told me to take it easy. While Charlie and Raymond unloaded everything else, they helped the girls put up the new curtains, and Tabatha had took the blanket and sheets home with her and washed them so that they would be soft and comfortable when Heather came home. Heather's room looked great after they made the bed. And I found pictures of Todd as a child playing on the beach, so I had put them in frames and hung them in Heather's room. Robert hooked up the new TV I bought for Heather's room. Sherry went to get lunch, and when she came back with sub sandwiches, she said that the Italian restaurant was sending dinner over around four to welcome Heather home. After everybody ate and we finished a few things, everyone left except Sherry.

She was off today so she hung out with us and played with Nicky. We talked all afternoon until Todd and Heather came home. We heard the SUV coming and Nicky was so excited that he went running out to meet them. Heather looked so great and was happy to be home. Todd helped her out of the car and she noticed that the cottage door had been painted. Heather smiled and said, "Todd, my door looks great. When did you have time to paint it? You've been at the hospital most of the time with me."

"I didn't paint it, Mother, but you have to thank Missy for getting it painted," Todd said.

Everyone noticed he called Heather "mother" but didn't say anything. As Heather walked into the house, her eyes filled with tears. And she looked at me and said, "It looks wonderful dear, but you shouldn't have. But I'm glad you did. This room needed painted for a long time, but I never had the chance to get it done."

Heather hugged me and I hugged her back. "I'm glad you like it. I wanted to do something special for you for all your kindness," I said.

I watched Heather go into her bedroom and she came back out in tears. "I have never seen such a beautiful bedroom before. I love the curtains and bedding and you got me a new bed. Bless you, my dear." And hugged me again.

Todd told Heather, "Mother, you need to rest. When you get up for dinner, you can go through the whole house."

Heather smiled and said, "Yes, son." And she went in her room and shut the door.

Sherry asked, "Heather, do you need any help?"

"No, I'm fine. I'm just going to rest awhile too. Thank you so much for everything." I gave her a hug.

I asked Sherry if she wanted to stay for dinner but she said no. She had things to do but she'll answer our call if we needed anything. I laid down for a nap and I was up before four when I heard a loud car pull in. It was the Italian restaurant bringing dinner. I thanked them and gave them a nice tip and sat everything on the counter. Heather got up around five, and I was just setting dinner out. Nicky went to help her in her chair and

Nicky talked during the whole meal. I cleaned up the kitchen while Todd, Nicky, and Heather watch TV. Then I told Nicky it was bedtime, but he wanted to show Heather his room first. Then when they came back, he said goodnight and gave Heather a hug and asked if she was going to be here when he gets up. And she gave him a hug and she promised that she would be. Heather excused herself, said she was tired and going to bed. Todd stayed the night with me and he stayed every night after that. We all fell into a happy family after about a few weeks.

I got up on Friday morning not feeling well, but Todd had gone to the hospital to see the chief of staff. And when he came back home, he announced that he was going back to work starting Monday. I told Todd that I was happy for him, and that I know he will be happier at the hospital since Heather was back to normal. I had a doctor's appointment that afternoon and I had been going by myself so that Todd would be with Heather, but today, he asked Heather if she and Nicky wanted to go also and we could eat dinner out afterward. But Heather said she had company coming and Nicky could stay with her if he wanted, but I told Heather that he needed to go with me so he could see Sherry at the hospital. We headed to the hospital, and I asked Todd, "Who's coming to see Heather? I noticed she put on a really nice outfit and put makeup on."

Todd said, "Robert's coming. He's bringing dinner for them that's why I wanted to come with you today. But I didn't want her to know that I knew what was going on."

I laughed. "You don't have a problem with her and Robert, do you?"

"No, not really. It's just that since she's been in the hospital, I want her to take it easy," Todd said.

"I think it's wonderful that she and Robert are interested in each other. She needs companionship and love," I said, smiling.

My doctor's appointment went well. He said that everything was on target but that I need to eat more. I had only gained sixteen pounds in this pregnancy, and the normal weight must be twenty-four to thirty pounds. Then we went to Cody's Steak House for dinner. I told Todd that I was selling the house in Texas and that I was going to fly down and make the arrangements, but he was concerned and asked if I could wait until after I have the baby and my blood pressure is back to normal, so I agreed to wait. I thought about what he asked and told him that I might wait until spring and sell both houses. We took our time over dinner so that Heather could enjoy her time with Robert. We got back around eight, and Robert had already left. Heather was in the kitchen having tea.

"How was your evening?" I asked.

Heather said, "It was good. How was your appointment?"

"It was good. Baby girl's on target," I answered.

Heather asked, "Have you pick out a name yet?"

"No, not yet. Nicky wants to name her Rocky. My mother's name was Sharon Michelle, and George's wife was Sophie, so I'm leaning toward Sophie Michelle. But I'm not for sure," I said.

"Why don't you name her after George instead? You could name her Georgia Michelle," Heather said.

"That's a pretty name," I agreed. "I'll have to write it down on my list."

"I'm going to bed. See you in the morning," Heather said and went to bed.

I had a restless night and woke up with my back hurting and an upset stomach. Todd asked if I was okay, and I said I was fine. As the day wore on, my back was getting worse.

Heather told Todd, "Maybe you should take her to the hospital."

"No, I just saw my doctor. I'll be okay. It was just a backache and pressure," I said.

Todd insisted on taking me and getting check out. He took me to the hospital. They took me straight back and put me on a monitor. Then the ER doctor came in and asked, "What was going on?"

"My back is hurting. It's like there's pressure on it," I told him.

Dr. Smith asked me, "How long has this been going on?"

"It started around two this morning," I answered.

Dr. Smith said, "You've been in labor since two this morning, and you're coming in just now."

"I'm not in labor. I have a backache," I said.

Dr. Smith said, "Well, the monitor says you're in labor."

I looked at Todd, and he smiled. "It looks like we're having a baby tonight."

Dr. Smith said, "We've page your doctor, and he's on the way in." Then he walked out.

I looked at Todd. "Am I stupid? I didn't know that I'm in labor."

Todd walked over, kissed me, and said, "You would be surprise how many women don't know there in labor until it's almost too late to make it to the hospital."

"It's too soon to have the baby. I'm not due for another eight weeks," I said.

Todd said, "She's ready now. It will be fine, and babies have their own time schedule. Don't worry, I'm not leaving your side. I promise."

Todd went out to the desk to use the phone and called Heather to tell her, but she said that she already knew and that Nicky was very excited about Rocky. Todd told me what Heather said about Rocky, and I laughed until the pain hit me. Todd said he was going to check on what was keeping the doctor, and as he left, Sherry came rushing in the room.

"I can't believe it! You're really early, but you'll be fine, and so will Susie Lou," she said.

I asked Sherry, "Can you stay with me? I'm really nervous and scared."

Sherry smiled. "Of course, I will. I'm not working tonight, and even if I were, I would be here for you. I just came by to visit my neighbor. He's in here with pneumonia, and I hate to say this, but I'm glad, or I'd be home and not here."

Dr. Culver and Todd walked in as the pain hit me. "It's okay, Missy, you're doing fine," Dr. Culver said as he looked at the monitor. "The nurse will be transferring you to labor and delivery, and I think we'll have a baby girl before the night is out."

They transferred me in no time, and the delivery nurse hooked me up on her monitor. Then she checked me to see how far along I was dilated. The nurse said, "You're at eight, so you're having this baby soon." She went out to tell the doctor, and he came in and said it was time to break the water, and that would move everything really fast. And it did. My contractions got harder and quicker instantly, and I asked the doctor if Sherry could also stay with me, and he said, "Sure, the more, the merrier." Sherry was on one side and Todd on the other, and within twenty minutes, my beautiful baby girl came into this world. I could hear her little cry. They brought her over so I can see. She was so tiny but beautiful. She weighed four pounds and four ounces, and they took her to the NICU unit for preemies.

"I want to go with her," I said.

"No, you're not able to go with her right now, but you will see her soon. I promise," Todd said.

"Do you want me to go and check on her for you?" Sherry asked.

"Yes, please let her know how much I love her," I said.

Sherry smiled and said, "I'll be back to check on you shortly." And out the room she went. Todd held my hand.

Then Dr. Culver said, "I think we have a slight problem."

"What's going on?" Todd asked.

Dr. Culver answered, "You have another baby coming. You were carrying twins, and we never realized it."

"But I'm not having any pain," I said. "There can't be another baby unless it's . . ."

Dr. Culver said, "He looks small, but he's alive."

I wasn't having any pain at all, but the doctor delivered him. He had a very weak cry, and they rushed in to work on him and rushed him out of the room.

"What's happening? Is he okay? Where are they taking him?" I kept asking.

Todd said, "They're taking care of him. He's very small. He needs care."

I drifted off into a fog. I could hear Todd calling my name but I couldn't answer him.

I came to, and the sun was shining in the window. My throat was so dry. I tried to speak, but nothing came out. I moved my hand and felt someone's hand. And then I heard Todd ringing the bell, calling the nurse and doctor. I could barely open my eyes, but I could see Todd and Sherry standing over me, looking serious.

"Water," I said.

Sherry gave me a few drops of water in my mouth.

Sherry said, "Slowly, Missy. You've been so sick. You need to take it easy. The doctors are on the way in."

Todd smiled and said, "Hey, beautiful, about time you woke up." He bent down and kissed me on the forehead.

Sherry gave me some more water. She said, "You gave us a scare, lady. How do you feel?"

"Where are my babies?" I whispered.

Todd said, "The babies are doing good. Baby girl has gained two ounces and baby boy has gained one ounce, but he's really little, he only weigh three pounds and one ounce at birth. But the doctors are very hopeful."

I tried to sit up, but I felt so weak. Sherry and Todd helped pull me up and raise my head as the doctors came in.

Dr. Culver said, "It's about time you wake up. I was getting worried about you. Your blood pressure went up sending you into preeclampsia, and we decided to put you into a medical coma until your blood pressure came down."

"How long have I been out?" I asked.

Dr. Culver said, "I thought you'd wake up a couple of days ago, how you feel?"

He listened to my heart and took my blood pressure, then he looked in my eyes and he bent my legs up and out. "Does anything hurt?" Dr. Culver asked.

I shook my head no, then I said, "I'm sore but not really in pain. Can I see my babies?"

Dr. Waters said, "You need to take it easy, but this doctor here will answer all your questions concerning your babies. This is Dr. Peterson. He's a pediatric preemie doctor. I'll check on you later this evening."

Dr. Peterson said, "I'm glad your awake. Your daughter is doing great. She's eating small amounts and gaining weight, but your baby boy is a lot smaller than his sister and he only weighs three pounds six ounces when he was born. He lost three ounces but has gained them back, plus one extra ounce. So he's doing better than I thought he would. He's almost a week old and if he continues to gain weight and learn to drink from a bottle, he will start gaining more." Dr. Peterson smiled and said, "I know it's hard, but you just have to be patient. If you're up for a ride to NICU, you can go and sit with them for a short time. You have to take care of yourself so that you'll be able to take care of them when they come home. I'll get the nurse to get you a wheelchair, and I'll check on you later this evening too."

Sherry helped me wash my face and brushed my hair. Then Todd and Sherry helped me in the wheelchair and took me to the NICU unit. Todd warned me. "Don't panic with all the tubes and wires, I'll be by your side the whole time."

I was shocked that the unit that Todd took me had several preemies, and they were wired up for sound and vital signs and heart monitors. Todd pushed me over to baby girl one Chambers and beside her was baby boy two Chambers. My daughter was so small and beautiful and was just perfect, but my baby boy was tiny, and he just was so quiet, but he was so beautiful too. They were in incubators, and I could put my hand into each one and touch my babies. I was totally in love. I turned to Todd. "Have you brought Nicky up to see the babies?"

Todd said, "No. With you being so sick, I didn't want to upset him. But now that you're awake, I'll bring him up tomorrow, okay?"

I shook my head and said, "Thank you, Todd." I stayed in the NICU for a short while. I was so weak. Todd took me back to my room and helped me in bed. And I fell asleep. I woke up later that afternoon and I heard Sherry talking to Todd about me.

"You have to tell her. You don't want her to find out about what we're doing behind her, back especially since she had the babies," Sherry said.

"I just can't tell her. Let her think everything's fine for now, until I have to tell her the truth. I don't want her to blame you," Todd said.

"She's going to be upset with the both of us. We've been going behind her back for some time now. I don't know that she'll forgive us," Sherry said.

I could see Todd putting his arms around Sherry.

My head was spinning. What was going on? What are they keeping from me? And why is Todd holding Sherry? Then it dawn on me. Sherry had said that she and Todd grew up together, and that everyone thought they would marry. Could it be that Todd doesn't love me and he's in love with Sherry? Todd walked over to me and looked down, and asked, "Missy, are you okay? Are you in pain? I see tears in your eyes."

I looked up at Todd, the man I was in love with, and my heart was breaking. But I said, "No, I'm fine. Can you take me to see the babies?"

"Maybe you need to rest longer," Todd said.

But I said, "No, I want to go now."

Todd smiled and said, "Okay, I'll get your chair. I'll be back in a minute. Sherry can you help Missy sat on the side of the bed?"

"Of course I will. I'll be here for you whenever you need me," Sherry said.

Sherry helped me to sat on the side of the bed, and Todd came in with a wheelchair and helped me into it and took me to see the babies. The nurse that was in the NICU unit asked if I had names pick out yet, but I told her no. I will start figuring names for them so she gave me a baby name book to look through. I sat with the twins for almost two hours. It broke my heart to leave them, but I was just too tired and weak to stay any longer. Todd helped me back in bed and he said that after I ate dinner, Heather will bring Nicky up to see me. So I ate some soup and drank some tea, but I couldn't do much. Sherry took the tray out of the room and I asked Todd if everything was okay. He and Sherry seemed off, but he said that everything is fine, and I heard Nicky coming down the hall, and Sherry opened the door. Nicky, Heather, and Robert came walking in. Nicky asked if I was okay, and I told him that I'm fine now that I got to see him. Heather gave me a hug and Todd helped Nicky up on the bed with me. Todd, Heather, Sherry, and Robert went out in the hallway to let me and Nicky talked. I showed him pictures of the babies and he asked if they had names, but I told him I have a book of names, maybe he can help me pick out names. So we looked through the names and tried out several, but we did more laughing than name picking.

Nicky asked, "Are you okay, Mommy? Are you sad about Robert and Shelly?"

I asked him, "What about Robert and Shelly, are they here?"

"No, they went to see George and Sophie," Nicky said.

I was in shock. Todd and Heather walked in, and I asked Todd, "What happened to Robert and Shelly?"

Todd stopped dead in his tracks. I asked, "Nicky said they went to visit George and Sophie, what happened?"

Heather asked Nicky to go with her to get coffee and ice cream, so after they left, Todd sat down on the bed and took my hand, and said, "They were killed in a boating accident when Heather was in the hospital. I was going to tell you, but you're blood pressure was up and I didn't want to upset you, so I decided to tell you after Heather came home. But then you went into labor and everything went out of control. The day you talked about going to Texas to sell the house, I had talked to Margaret that morning, and asked her not to say anything until you saw the doctor, and I had a chance to see what he thought. I'm sorry, Missy, I know how much Robert meant to you, but I was trying to protect you. Sherry said that I need to tell you, but I wasn't sure if you could handle it with your health and the babies being premature."

At least I knew now that it wasn't what I thought, but he should have told me. I said, "I understand you trying to protect me, but I had a right to know. I cared about both of them, but especially Shelly, we've been friends since I moved to Texas, and I was really close with her family. I need to call momma Harper."

Todd said, "I didn't realize you and Shelly were so close, I was more concern about how you would react over Robert."

"You had nothing to worry about when it came to Robert, he showed his true colors, and I only hope he was good to Shelly," I said.

Todd kissed me. "Am I forgiven?"

I smiled, and said, "Yes, but don't keep things from me."

I called Shelly's mom, Harper, and they talked for over thirty minutes. Harper said that Shelly and Robert got married and was very happy, but then Shelly found out that she had stage three lung cancer, and so they decided to go on a fishing trip before she started chemo and radiation, but the doctors said it would only prolong her life a few months, so maybe this was god's plan. Then she got off the phone.

Sherry came in. "Are you mad at me? I'm sorry."

"Yes, were good. I'm grateful for all you do for me and Nicky and the twins," I said.

The doctor came in after Sherry left, and told her that baby girl is doing wonderful, and baby boy gained two ounces in two days, and if he stayed on track, he would be going home in a few weeks, but that baby girl will most likely go home by the end of next week. After the doctor left, I got the baby book and started looking up for names, and I had decided that I was naming my baby girl, Harper Michelle Chambers, and my baby boy, Harley George Chambers. I got in my wheelchair and was almost to the door, when Todd, Heather, and Nicky came in, and Todd asked, "where are you going in such a hurry?"

I smiled, and said, "I want to show our twins off, Harley George and Harper Michelle, to Heather and Nicky."

Todd smiled, and said, "You hear that Nicky? Let's go and see your baby brother and baby sister."

And Nicky said, "Come on, Mom! Let's go and see them."

"Oh, what beautiful names. Let's go see the babies," Heather said.

The nurse motioned for me and Todd to come in the NICU unit, and Heather and Nicky stood by the big window so that they could see all the babies in the unit. The nurse moved the rocking chair over to the window and told me to sit, and she would get baby girl Chambers for me to hold. I told her we had names, and she wrote both names down so that she could do new name tags for their little beds. I was so ready to hold her, so I got out of the wheelchair and sat in the rocker, and Sandy the nurse got

Harper out and laid her on my chest, and the nurse brought me a warm baby blanket to cover her with. Heather and Nicky could see how beautiful she is, and Nicky was blowing her kisses. The nurse brought Todd a chair to sit by me. She was so tiny, but she loved cuddling and little kisses. Todd took pictures of us, and the nurse asked Todd, "Would you like to hold little Ms. Harper?" But he said, "No, I'll wait, let her momma hold her." Then she told him, "You need to hold Ms. Harper so that I can bring Harley to his momma."

I couldn't believe it, I was getting to hold both my babies. Nurse Sandy took Harper from me and handed her to Todd, and she help him get situated. And then she went and got Harley out of his incubator and brought him over to me, she help me hold him, he was so much small that Harper, even though she was also tiny, but he weighed a pound and a half less than Harper. He cried out and I got scared, but the nurse said it's good for them to cry or coo. I help Harley for about ten minutes than nurse Sandy said before I return him to his bed, so that he wouldn't lose body temperature. I gave him kisses and he just cooed and snuggled like he didn't want to leave me. The nurse said if I felt like it, I could come back in forty-five minutes and feed him, so I told her I'd be back. I got to hold Harper again, then it was time for her to go back to her little bed. Sandy said that she had just fed Harper when we came, but after I fed Harley, I could also try feeding Harper, so I told her I'd be back, and Todd took me to my room. Robert was there with food for everyone, including me, it was Sub sandwiches, and I was hungry. The nurse came in to tell me I was going to go to x-ray for a CAT scan in a few minutes, but I told her I couldn't because I was going to get to feed the babies, so she said she would call down and ask them to come later this evening. After we ate, Robert took Heather and Nicky home, and I almost cried to see Nicky leaving, but he told me I'd be okay, he'll see me tomorrow, and gave me a hug and kiss, then he was gone. Todd took me to the nursery and I got to hold Harley and feed him, but he only took a small amount. Nurse Sandy said that it's normal, and that they would tube feed him from eight o'clock in the evening to eight in the morning. Then I fed Harper and she ate good, she drank almost two ounces. And after the nurse took her, I went to my room and then the transport came and took me for my x-rays. After I got back to my room, Todd wasn't anywhere to be found, so I turned on the TV and fell asleep. The lab tech woke me at five in the morning, and Todd was asleep in the recliner in my room. The lab tech said he's been in that chair every night since I got here. That morning, I told Todd that he needed to go home at night and get some rest, and that I was fine by myself and that he needed rest, but he said that as long as I was in the hospital, he would be there with me. We went and spent time with the twins. Harper was getting stronger and growing each day, and Harley was slowly gaining weight, but he loved his visits and snuggle time. On the way back to my room, the chief of staff ask Todd when he could return to work, and Todd told him he would let him know as soon as he could. After I got back into bed, I started to tell Todd that he could go ahead and work when my doctor came in.

"How is my patient today?" Dr. Culver asked.

"I'm feeling better, and I got to hold and feed the twins," I said.

"Your x-ray looked good. I'm going to release you on Friday from here, but if you want to stay here until they go home, I could possibly do that," Dr. Culver said.

"No, I don't want to take up a bed that someone else will need. I will go home and drive in each day until they come home," I said.

"Dr. Peterson talked like the girl will be sent home over the weekend, and the boy will be in here longer, but once he starts gaining weight, it will go quick," Dr. Culver said. "I'll let you rest and check on you tomorrow."

"Todd, I don't have a crib or hardly any baby things, what am I going to do?" I asked.

Todd said, "Don't worry, it's being taken care of." He smiled, and said, "This wasn't the way I planned it." Then Todd got down on one knee, and asked, "Will you marry me, Missy? I love you, and I love Nicky, Harper, and Harley. I promise to make you happy and be a good husband and father."

I was up out of bed and ran into his arms, and we both hit the floor. "Of course, I will marry you. I love you silly, I want nothing more than to become your wife."

The nurse came in to bring my medication, and she yelled for help, but we both just started laughing. Two other nurses came rushing in and helped me and Todd up, they were asking if I was okay, if I was dizzy, or if I tripped, but I told them I just got engaged, and they started laughing too and congratulate us. After all the commotion calmed down, we went back to the nursery and news travels quick in the hospital. Nurse Sandy congratulated us as we walked in, and Dr. Peterson was there, and he said he was very happy for us. Then he said, "Baby Harley is doing good. He now weighs four pounds and four ounces, so if he keeps this up, I'm sending them home next Friday barring no complications. I had thought about sending Harper home, but I find twins responds well with the other twin close by. You can hold them and feed them whenever you want, okay?"

"Okay and thank you, Dr. Peterson," I said, and Todd thanked him too, and he left. We held both babies and fed them, then when they fell asleep, we came back to my room. When we walked in, there was flowers, candy, balloons all over the room, and the bed was made and had rose petals all over it, then there was a huge white cupcake with pink hearts and candy kisses on it, with "Will you marry me?" and "I Do" on the cupcake.

Sherry walked out of the bathroom, and she said, "Surprise!"

I hugged her. She said, "I can't believe you already asked her, after you asked me to do this to surprise her with it."

Todd looked sheepish. "Got caught up in the moment."

Sherry hugged me. "I'm so happy for you."

After everybody left, several nurses came in and congratulated us. Then Todd said he would be back later and left, so I asked the nurse if I could take a shower. She said yes, but if I needed help, she said I just need to pull the emergency call in the bathroom. So I got a shower and put on a clean gown and got in bed and was almost asleep when Todd came back. He gave me a kiss and said, "Hello, beautiful, I missed you."

I asked where he went. He explained that he talked to the chief of the hospital and took off three more months. That way, he could help me with the babies, and we could get married and get everything in order before he came back to work. So he said that it is fine with Dr. Reynolds and he also sent his blessings. I got release and spent most of my time at the hospital the following week, and sure enough, Harper and Harley was released the following Friday. When they arrived at Heather's, the driveway was full of cars, and there were over thirty visitors there from town and the hospital. I was so excited to bring the babies home that I forgot to buy cribs and get them sat up, but Todd said that everything was ready for them and told me not to worry. Everyone passed Harley and Harper around, then I told Todd it was time to put them down, so I followed him into my bedroom where there was two portable cribs, and we laid them down and they went to sleep. There were all kinds of food to eat, so we ate, and everybody left. Then Todd said, "I have a surprise for you. Is it okay to leave Harley and Harper here for a few minutes while I take you to see your surprise?"

I said, "I don't want to put too much on Heather."

Robert said, "We can handle it, they'll be fine."

I said, "Okay," and Todd help me out to the SUV, and I thought maybe we were going to Todd's house, but instead, he went out to the main highway. "Where are we going, Todd?" I asked.

Todd smiled. "You'll see in a few minutes." And we went past the town, and Todd turned into a gravel driveway. I knew this place; it was George's house. After we got parked, Todd helped me out of the SUV, and we went inside the house. The whole house had been painted. Every room, instead of the gray walls, was freshly painted off-white and trimmed in bright white, similar to what I had pick for Heather, except I had told Robert that Heather's favorite color was light sea foam blue, and even though it turned out great, I preferred off-white walls. The house was beautiful, and everything was polished and clean, and Todd took me upstairs to George's master bedroom. It was painted a light lavender color with new white curtains in it and an adjoining sitting room. There was a new bedroom set in there, and the sitting room was turned into a nursery painted white with Mickey and Minnie Mouse decorations. There were two round cribs, one done in Mickey for Harley, and the other crib was done in Minnie for Harper. I told Todd, "I love it! It's beautiful. It's perfect. But when did you have time for all this?"

Todd said, "I'd had help. You and the kids mean everything to me. I'll always have time for you and our family. Do you like the house?"

I smiled. "Yes, I love the house."

Todd said, "Good, 'cause this is where we are going to live until you want something different, okay? I hope you didn't mind me making that decision. I know you probably would have liked to choose the colors and furniture, but I wanted you and the babies to come home and be comfortable. Between Heather, Robert, and Sherry, we got everything done yesterday, and Sherry stocked the refrigerator and cabinets and got anything we need for the babies and Nicky. I love you so much that in a few days, we'll sit down and pick a wedding date and make all the plans that you want, okay?"

I smiled, reached up, and kissed Todd. "Let's go get our children and bring them home, okay?"

Todd smiled and said, "Yes, let's go get our children and bring them to our new home."

We went to Heather's and got Nicky and the babies and came home. After we got everybody home and settled in bed, Todd told me that they kept everything that was in the house and they packed up and put it in the attic and basement so that when I was ready, I could go through it and decide what I wanted to do with it. We went to bed and Todd held me, and I wanted him to make love, but he said I needed to rest and build my strength. So he just held me while I slept until I was back to health. I slept so good that I didn't hear Harley when he woke, so Todd got up and changed him and fed him a bottle and put him down again. We fell into a routine, taking care of Harley and Harper, with Nicky's help being the big brother, which he took seriously. Todd went back to work part-time so that he could help me with the kids. We set a wedding date, and I slowly went through George's and Sophie's things. I kept some of them, but then I sent some to goodwill.

One day, when I was going through some boxes in the attic, I came across Sophie's wedding dress. It was beautiful. It was ivory color with long sleeves done in Italian lace and a low-cut neckline with a matching veil. There was a white jewelry box with a pearl necklace, earrings, and a diamond bracelet and a hat box that held Sophie's bridal bouquet with silk white roses, purple orchids, pearls, and silver streamers. When Sherry came over, I asked her if she thought it would be okay if I wore the dress and veil, and Sherry encouraged me to wear them all and use the bouquet. They all looked perfect and beautiful, and she thought I'd be beautiful in them also. As we were putting everything back in its boxes, Sherry found an envelope with my name on it. It was George's handwriting, and I sat on a trunk and read his letter:

Sept. 21, 1982

My dearest Melissa,

You have been my saving grace since I lost Sophie. If it wasn't for you, I would have joined Sophie, but you kept me going. In a year's time, you should have forgotten me and gone on with your life, but instead, we became family. Sophie and I talked about having a daughter but never were that lucky until the day I met you and my world fell apart, but you kept me going. I just wish Sophie could have known you. You're an amazing girl, and the unconditional love you gave to a total stranger was so amazing that I want you to have this house so that one day, you'll be as happy as me, and Sophie was here. This is where we lived when we had our son and raised him. Then we moved to Texas so we would be close to him in college, and after we lost him, we just couldn't come back to the memories. I know I've only known you for six months, but I know one day, when I'm gone, you could be happy here and find love and build a family here. Do whatever you want with the house and its contents. It's yours now, so enjoy it. You'll never know how much I love you and wish we would have known you before Sophie passed away. You have such a gentle heart just like my Sophie. You remind me of her at times. There is a box of pictures, and in there, you'll find the deed to the house, and I set up a trust to keep the taxes paid each year in case I got senile and forgot, so it's all in your name know. When we go to Florida next year, I'll show you the place. Thank you for being a great friend, and I think of you as family and always will.

Love,

George

When Todd came home, I showed him the letter, and he was amazed by it. He said, "Not only did you save George's life, you gave me my life. I felt like my life was nothing when I lost my best friend in the ER and couldn't even save his children. I had just given up until I saw you standing there looking at fireworks. The moment I saw your face, I knew you were something special, and George knew it also." Todd locked me in his arms and said, "I love you so much. I am the luckiest man on earth, and we have George looking over us as we build our lives." Then Todd looked up and said, "Thank you, George, for bringing Missy into my life and heart." Then he kissed me.

Later that evening, Todd looked at George's letter and noticed the date. He was amazed but not surprised that Missy made such a difference in George's life. I walked into the bedroom where Todd was sitting, holding the letter, and I said, "It was sweet of him to do this for me and Nicky. He was a wonderful man and the best father I could have ever had. I just wish he was here to see us." Todd said, "I think he's watching over us, and I think he'll be happy knowing you found love." Then he pointed out the date. Todd said, "George said in the letter you were amazing back then, and in a year, you grew into a daughter to him. That is amazing. I'm very happy that you made a difference in George's life. He was a very lucky man, and so were you."

We talked most of the night about George and what a difference he made to my life and Nicky's. I told Todd everything about my life: how my mom passed away, how my dad forgot me when he married, and that George was a gift. I smiled. "He loved me unconditionally, and when Nicky came along, he loved him and would do anything for either one of us." I sighed. "I missed him so much, it still hurts. George's gift of love is what made me who I am today. He was like a father to me but also my best friend. And when things get tough for me, I talk to him, and it's like he hears me and steers me in the right direction. And I know you think I'm crazy, but I feel he's with me, watching over me and Nicky and now the twins and you," I said then laughed. "He and Sophie are our guardian angels. I know everything will be all right."

We set the wedding date on December 24, Christmas Eve, at the house. I asked Sherry to be my maid of honor, and Nicky was the ring bearer. Robert walked me down the aisle, and it seemed like the whole town came. It was one big party. I wore Sophie's wedding dress and wore her jewelry and carried her bouquet. Sherry gave me a locket for something new, and I put George and Sophie's pictures in it and pinned it to the bridal bouquet. Sophie's dress was old, and Heather gave me her lace gloves that she wore with her wedding dress for something barrowed. Todd gave me a beautiful sapphire engagement ring as something new. Sherry and Heather gave me a bridal shower two weeks before the wedding, and I got a beautiful lingerie to take on our three-day honeymoon at the bed and breakfast in town because we didn't want to be too far away from the kids. The night before we got married, Heather asked us over for dinner and to talk. So when we got there, Robert asked Todd for Heather's hand in marriage. They were so cute. You could tell how much they loved each other. Todd gave his blessing, and we had a good dinner, and Sherry came over around eight with her sister, Danna, and Christy, and me and the twins were staying the night with Heather. Todd and Nicky was having a guy's night, so after Todd and Nicky left, Christy did all of our nails, and Danna, was coming in the morning to do our hair, and makeup. We stayed up most of the night and had a great time, and Sherry helped me with my dress and to get ready. Christy's husband Joseph, showed up at noon to take pictures of us, and he also took pictures during the wedding and reception. Everything was beautiful and romantic, and after Joseph took pictures, a white horse and white carriage showed up to take me to the house, along with two other carriages to take everybody else. Heather and Robert took the twins in the car so that they could get them settled before the service starts. When the carriage pulled up, Raymond and Charlie helped me out and walked me into the house. The formal living room was turned into a wedding chapel. There were white and lavender flowers and ribbons on the chairs and tables and candles everywhere. We had never talked about wedding colors, but I guessed Sherry must have done all of these. It was beautiful, and there was soft music playing, and there were a lot of people already there seated. I went into the drawing room to check on Harper and Harley. I could hear them fussing, but Danna and Christy were with them, and Nicky was helping out. Nicky looked up and smiled. "You look beautiful, Mommy. Why are you all dressed up?"

"Don't you remember I'm marrying Todd today?" I said.

Nicky asked, "You have to dress up to do that?"

"Well, yes, look at you, you're all dressed up and quite handsome let me tell you, so I wanted to dress up also," I said.

Nicky smiled. "I am handsome, Mommy, but I'm glad I don't have to wear a dress."

I laughed. "I'm glad you don't have to either, sweetie. Are you ready to do this?"

Nicky said, "Okay, let's get this show on the road."

I laughed. "Where did you hear that from?"

"Todd. Mommy, can I call Todd daddy after you marry him?" Nicky asked.

"I think so. Maybe we better ask, but I think he'll be okay with it," I said.

The twins had fell asleep, and Sherry came in looking for us. "It's almost time. You ready?"

I smiled. "Yes, I'm ready." Nicky said, "Me too."

The wedding was beautiful. There were lots of pictures and good wishes and a great reception. I looked at Todd and smiled. "I love you." Todd kissed me. "I love you, too."

The End

Lightning Source UK Ltd.
Milton Keynes UK
UKHW010800040119
334855UK00002B/31/P

9 781984 573650